VICTORIAN
MANSION
FLOWER SHOP
MYSTERIES

Best Laid Plants

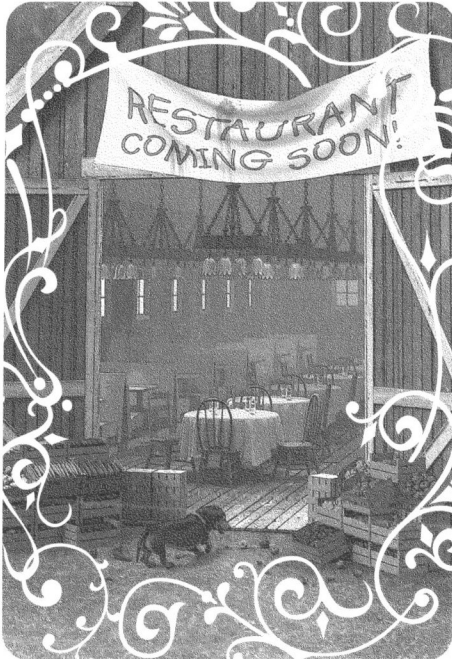

Katy Lee

Books in the Victorian Mansion Flower Shop Mysteries series

A Fatal Arrangement
Bloomed to Die
The Mistletoe Murder
My Dearly Depotted
Digging Up Secrets
Planted Evidence
Loot of All Evil
Pine and Punishment
Herbal Malady
Deadhead and Buried
The Lily Vanishes
A Cultivated Crime
Suspicious Plots
Weeds of Doubt
Thorn to Secrecy
A Seedy Development
Woes By Any Other Name
Noel Way Out
Rooted in Malice
Absent Without Leaf
Dormant Lies
Best Laid Plants
Pocket Full of Deadly
To Hive and to Hold

Library of Congress-in-Publication Data
Best Laid Plants / by Katy Lee
p. cm.
ISBN: 978-1-64025-842-6
I. Title
2019942860

AnniesFiction.com
(800) 282-6643
Victorian Mansion Flower Shop Mysteries™
Series Creators: Shari Lohner, Janice Tate
Editor: Elizabeth Morrissey
Cover Illustrator: Bob Kayganich

10 11 12 13 14 | Printed in China | 9 8 7 6 5

1

"Quiet on set! And we're rolling."

After a few weeks on location with *Restaurant Restarts*, a reality television show filming in Turtle Cove, Washington, Kaylee Bleu no longer felt a thrill of excitement when the director announced that cameras were filming. Instead, she continued digging a hole in the soil where she'd soon place another heirloom tomato seedling, glancing up only occasionally to watch the proceedings.

"Welcome back to *Restaurant Restarts*," host Gabe Forester said in his jovial, made-for-TV voice. "We're on beautiful Orcas Island, bringing new life to the Madrona Grove Farm and Orchard. It was once a rundown, ramshackle property, but by the time we're done with the barn and gardens, it'll be the island's premier farm to table restaurant!" Gabe flashed a grin crammed with gleaming white teeth and gestured behind him to an empty pasture bearing only a few patches of dried grass. "So, just how are we going to turn this barren wasteland into a profitable, sustainable eatery? Hard work, creativity, and a little magic." He winked.

Magic is right, Kaylee thought wryly, raising an eyebrow at the mass of high-tech cameras, microphones, teleprompters, playback screens, and other equipment set up opposite the "barren wasteland." Dozens of crew members milled around, as did a few locals who had been invited to take part in the show, including Kaylee and the rest of the Petal Pushers garden club: Mary Bishop, Jessica Roberts, and DeeDee Wilcox.

Accompanied by Kaylee's adorable dachshund, Bear, who was basking in the warm May sunshine nearby, the women were all on their hands and muddy knees in a garden plot beside the farm's massive red barn, enjoying the change of pace from their respective businesses—Kaylee owned a florist shop called The Flower Patch, where Mary worked as a part-time designer, while Jessica ran the bakery next door, Death by Chocolate, and DeeDee sold mystery books at her shop, Between the Lines. The women had volunteered their past few Sunday afternoons to help plant flower beds and vegetable patches around the property. With the tight filming schedule, apparently there wasn't enough time for the farm to mature naturally, so the Petal Pushers were helping it along. It was part of the hard work Gabe had mentioned, though Kaylee doubted their contributions were what he'd meant.

"Speaking of magic," Gabe continued, "there is an enchanted feeling on Orcas Island, and I've been in awe of its natural beauty ever since I stepped off the boat."

"Boat, my foot," Mary muttered just loud enough for the other Petal Pushers to hear. "We all know he arrived by helicopter less than an hour ago even though the rest of the crew hauled their gear over last month by ferry."

"At least he got here in plenty of time to have his hair varnished into a helmet." DeeDee brushed her own blonde locks out of her eyes. "I haven't seen a single strand budge in this wind."

"You have to admit, he's even more handsome in person than he is on TV," Jessica said, a grin on her pixielike face. "Mila would be so jealous right now."

Kaylee chuckled, sure that if Jessica's twentysomething daughter didn't live on the mainland, she would have been lingering around the set since the time filming had begun a few weeks prior, as many other area residents had been doing. Thinking about how long the crew had already been working, she said, "It's funny, isn't it? I've seen several episodes of this show, and I always thought that Gabe was on-site from start to finish for every renovation. Turns out he just swoops in from California for a few days at the very end after everyone else has done all the work."

"Well, like Gabe just said"—Mary waved her trowel like a wand—"it's magic."

Everyone laughed, then DeeDee nudged Kaylee with an elbow. "Didn't you say Reese knows Gabe somehow? He must be excited to see his famous friend."

Kaylee glanced toward the far end of the barn, where her boyfriend, Reese Holt, was climbing a ladder, paintbrush in hand. "They went to college together, but Reese has honestly said more to me about the new windows he's installing than about Gabe."

"He's done an amazing job constructing new windows to match the old ones." DeeDee reached for another bell pepper plant to place in the soil. "It's a pity so many of the original windows rotted or were broken after the bank foreclosed on the farm."

"Now that he's painting them, I can't even tell the difference between the old and new ones," Kaylee said admiringly, proud of her talented—not to mention handsome—beau. "Although I think the showrunners told him to leave at least one of them bare so that Gabe can finish it."

"Just like the corner of the barn roof left undone so that Gabe can 'repair' it on camera?" Mary rolled her eyes. "I'm sorry to say it, but I think ignorance was bliss when it came to watching this show. Now that I see how the sausage gets made, I'm not sure I'm as big a fan."

"I'm reserving judgment until they edit it all together," DeeDee said, tamping soil around the base of her pepper plant. "The wedding they have planned for the grand finale will certainly be worth tuning in to see—especially for the gorgeous flowers from The Flower Patch."

"Josh and Savannah are a very nice couple from Eastsound,"

Mary said, her tone warming considerably. "Josh's dad, Preston Rutherford, is the president of the Orcas Island Historic Preservation Council."

"The council does such good work on the island," DeeDee said admiringly. "For instance, a Native American burial ground was uncovered near Steely Bay a few years ago during the early stages of a development. The council fought the investors all the way to court to protect the land. Fortunately, historic preservation won."

"Josh mentioned that he's hoping to follow in his father's footsteps on the council someday." Kaylee brushed a strand of her long, dark hair out of her eyes. "And Savannah expressed interest in helping Mary at the senior center. It's so nice that young islanders want to be involved, isn't it? I really enjoyed getting to know them during our wedding consultation last week."

Mary put a hand on her hip. "You mean the meeting the showrunners want us to repeat so they can capture it on camera?"

Jessica sighed melodramatically. "Too bad it's not someone we know getting married."

Kaylee caught the sparkle of teasing in her friend's almond-shaped eyes and waved her hand dismissively. "Reese and I are just dating," she said sternly, though she felt an electric thrill at Jessica's implication. "That's all."

Jessica nodded toward Reese. "Does he know that? Because judging by the way he's looking at you, I think he's hearing wedding bells."

Seeing that Reese did, in fact, have his twinkling blue eyes fixed on her, Kaylee beamed at him and waved, receiving a heart-fluttering grin in return before he continued with his work. Her smile wilted slightly as she thought of something. "He hasn't even told me he loves me, let alone mentioned marriage. And considering he's the one who got left at the altar by his ex, I don't think it's my place to bring it up."

"Technically I think Nicole broke their engagement months before the actual wedding day," Mary said as she dug a hole for a basil plant. "But I see your point." She paused with her trowel mid-scoop. "You aren't worried he still has feelings for her, are you?"

"No way is that possible." Jessica looked entirely aghast at the idea. "That look he just gave you? That's not a look a guy gives a girl when he's pining for somebody else."

"I can't argue with that," DeeDee chimed in. "He's head over work boots for you, Kaylee."

Although heartened by her friends' proclamations, Kaylee found herself growing distracted by activity near the barn. Reese was descending the ladder again, though he no longer had a carefree expression on his face. Instead, he appeared suddenly wary as Gabe approached him, a cameraman following close behind.

"And now I'd like to introduce a familiar face here on the island," the television host was saying. He chuckled. "Familiar to me, anyway. Our on-site craftsman, Reese Holt, is a buddy from my college days. It's nice to see he still bears the proof that he was once one of us." Gabe gestured at Reese's trademark Los Angeles Dodgers baseball hat. "You can take the boy out of L.A., but you can't take the L.A. out of the boy—isn't that right, pal?"

Reese tipped the brim of his cap. "The Dodgers will always have my allegiance, but my heart belongs here now." His gaze shifted beyond Gabe to Kaylee, and he smiled before ducking off camera and strolling toward the barn entrance.

"Come on back here, Reese," Gabe called after him. "Isn't it time to let bygones be bygones?" When Reese didn't react, Gabe remained still, a blank expression on his face, before finally yelling, "Cut!"

The host stomped off to a shaded area, and Kaylee thought

she heard him mutter something about the take being useless, but she was too far away to pick up all the words. There was one word she was focused on, however: what had he meant about bygones?

"Take five, everyone!" director Garth Sloan announced, an edge of irritation in his voice. He ran a hand over his balding pate, which was a stark contrast to his bushy salt-and-pepper beard. "When we come back, we'll do the Georgine Snowbird interview."

"Georgine Snowbird?" Kaylee repeated. "Is she a local?" Having moved to Orcas Island only a few years previously to take over The Flower Patch from her retiring grandmother, Bea Lyons, Kaylee wasn't as familiar with the island's residents as her friends who'd lived there much longer.

DeeDee nodded. "She's from the Lummi tribe."

"Really?" Kaylee's interest ramped up a notch. Her father, Chayton, was Quinault, another Native American tribe from the Pacific Northwest.

"Her ancestors have been on the island for generations and she lives close to the farm, so she's being interviewed about the history of Madrona Grove," DeeDee continued. "Or, I guess, about the land that was here long before any buildings were built on it."

"As if the more modern history weren't interesting enough," Jessica said with a sly grin, alluding to some criminal activity that had taken place on the property not many years before and resulted in the bank foreclosing on the farm. "I wonder if the Vanguards knew anything about it before they bought it at auction."

Mary chuckled. "I doubt anything would have deterred Matt from buying this place."

Recent transplants from California, Matt and Vanessa Vanguard had purchased Madrona Grove sight unseen, then swiftly relocated to Orcas Island with the intention of turning the property into a farm to table restaurant where, as Matt said, "you can see the farm from the table." Having gotten to know the couple over the past few weeks, Kaylee had been impressed by Matt's passion—he was an amateur farmer, but what he lacked in experience, he made up for in enthusiasm. Vanessa, the chef, was more reserved than her husband, but Kaylee had enjoyed spending time with her as the Petal Pushers helped plan and plant the gardens that would eventually fuel the restaurant's menu.

"Okay, everyone, break's over," Garth called over a megaphone from his seat in a director's chair beneath an oversize black umbrella. "Gabe, go to your mark. Ms. Snowbird, please join him."

Pausing in her planting, Kaylee watched a woman of about sixty with a mature but unlined face unhurriedly step up beside Gabe. The woman's sleek, black hair was parted in the middle and pulled into a simple braid down her back. She wore a woven coat featuring colorful stripes of varying thicknesses, and the back was emblazoned with a large eagle icon. Georgine focused on Gabe, but he gazed pointedly upward and shielded his face from the bright sun, a scowl on his unnaturally tanned face.

"Quiet on set," Garth said, ignoring Gabe's dramatic body language. "Cameras rolling. Action."

A forced smile replaced Gabe's glower as he squared his shoulders and addressed the camera. "I'm joined now by Georgine Snowbird, an expert on local history. Ms. Snowbird, please tell us more about the original inhabitants of Madrona Gr—" Before even finishing the sentence, Gabe let his artificially jovial expression drop. He shielded his face again and yelled, "Cut! Can someone get me a little shade? Don't you people see the sun shining in my eyes? I can't be squinting during an interview."

Garth leaped up from his chair and edged around a small monitor that showed the camera's feed. "If I've said it once, I've said it a hundred times, Gabe. I call the cues. Not you."

"Then do your job, Garth. Unless you're too relaxed under your little umbrella." Gabe's sharp glare shifted to the makeup artist, a young woman with stylishly short hair and cat-eye glasses. "Suzy, get me my sunglasses. It's too bright out here. And a water too while you're at it."

Suzy visibly tensed, but she did Gabe's bidding without vocal complaint. While the makeup artist scrambled toward the row of trailers set up behind the barn, Gabe retreated to his shaded spot under the barn's eaves.

The Petal Pushers exchanged glances. "Poor girl," Mary mouthed, then returned her focus to the row of herbs she'd started planting.

"I guess we're taking another five. Nino, was that as disastrous as it looked?" Garth asked the camera operator, a short, burly man named Nino Demarco.

"Nah," Nino replied casually, scratching at the dark stubble on his cheeks. "But Gabe will have to actually finish a sentence for the next take to be usable."

"Let's reposition the camera so he's not squinting into the sun anymore. If having his face shadowed is the price he's willing to pay for a little shade, so be it." Garth checked a clipboard. "Okay, after Ms. Snowbird's oral history, we'll bring out the Vanguards to interview."

The show's creator and producer—a well-dressed, energetic man with angular features named Sawyer Hawkins—nodded. "We can really play off their reaction to what the shaman woman says. Nino, make sure you get in tight on their faces. I want to make sure we capture their fear."

Kaylee frowned as she overheard their discussion. *Why on earth would Matt and Vanessa be scared after hearing anything Georgine has to say? And why does it sound like these guys want them to be?*

Garth glanced toward Georgine, who was still standing stoically in front of the camera. "Ms. Snowbird, don't go far. We'll pick right up with you when we start rolling."

Georgine replied with a single solemn nod, then said, "For the record, I am not a shaman. My grandfathers were, but I am simply an herbalist and storyteller of the history of my people."

"Mm-hmm, yeah," the director said distractedly as he returned to a conversation with Nino and Sawyer about technical aspects of the day's shooting schedule.

Eager to meet another plant enthusiast, Kaylee decided to take advantage of the break to introduce herself to Georgine. She grabbed Bear's leash and stepped carefully out of the garden, leading her dog over to the stoic older woman.

"Ms. Snowbird?" Kaylee smiled as Georgine gave a single nod. "My name is Kaylee Bleu, and this is Bear." Her dog panted blithely at her feet and cocked his head as if in greeting.

"Hello," Georgine answered.

"That's a lovely coat you have on," Kaylee said. "Did someone in your tribe make it?"

"Yes, long ago. It was my mother's. The eagle on the back is the emblem of our nation."

Kaylee glanced down and saw that the same emblem decorated a small leather pouch in the woman's hand. "Is that for your herbs?"

Georgine loosened the strings of the cinched sack and poured the contents into her palm. "Dried lavender to calm my nerves. There is trouble here."

"Trouble?" Kaylee echoed. She brushed a lock of hair out of her face as a fresh gust of sea wind hit her. She felt a chill. The timing of the gust and Georgine's nebulous statement were just a coincidence—right?

Georgine lifted her chin and took a deep breath, but didn't elaborate on her comment.

Brushing off the eerie moment, Kaylee went on. "I'm a florist. I own The Flower Patch in Turtle Cove." Technically she was more than a florist—she held a PhD in plant taxonomy, had years of experience as a professor at the University of Washington, and occasionally served as a forensic botany expert for the local sheriff's department—but she didn't feel that someone as reserved as Georgine would care about her credentials. "Do you grow your own botanicals?"

"Yes. I grow a variety of herbs and plants, most for healing and peace of mind. My family before me has always provided medicine to our people."

Intrigued, Kaylee said, "If it's not being too forward, I would love to visit your garden and learn about what you have growing." Georgine hummed a noncommittal response as she returned the dried lavender to her sack, and Kaylee wasn't sure if it meant to come by or not. "My background is in science, but the use of herbs and plants as part of spiritual healing is certainly an interesting concept."

Georgine aimed a level gaze at Kaylee. "My grandfather was the last shaman of my people. I simply carry on the knowledge of the plants. I have no powers. If you want a magic show, you'll have to look elsewhere."

"Let's go, people!" Garth bellowed through his megaphone just a few feet away, startling Kaylee and eliciting a sharp yip from Bear. "We don't have all day. Places!"

Kaylee hurried out of the camera's line of sight, keeping Bear's leash short so he stayed close. Before she went back to the garden, she paused for a moment to watch Gabe, who was gazing admiringly at himself in a mirror Suzy held.

With a final approving nod, Gabe strode to his new mark

and smiled smugly at the camera, which had been moved a few feet so that Gabe was out of the sun. "That wasn't so hard, was it, Garth?"

Rolling her eyes, Suzy stomped past Kaylee, muttering, "There's only so much I can hide with makeup. He won't be able to pretend he's in his twenties for much longer."

Garth instructed Nino to start rolling, then indicated for the host to restart his interview with Georgine.

Gabe ignited his megawatt smile for the camera. "There is such a rich history on Orcas Island, especially when it comes to the Native American tribes who lived here long ago. We're pleased to have Georgine Snowbird from the Lummi Tribe with us to share all about her people. Welcome, Georgine."

"Thank you." Georgine said, yet offered no smile. "But I am not here to share about my people's past. Instead, it is a warning I give."

Kaylee swallowed hard, a cold sensation creeping into her middle.

"The spirits of the land are not happy you are here. They want you all to leave." Georgine stared directly into Gabe's eyes, her gaze steely. "Get out before it is too late."

2

Gabe laughed nervously and cleared his throat. "Sounds spooky."

"No." Georgine shook her head gravely. "Not spooky. I am not trying to scare you with ghost stories. This is real. The people have spoken."

"The people?" Gabe glanced at the camera, suppressing a smirk. "Your people?"

"No, our enemies from long ago." Georgine stood up straighter, her shoulders squaring off. "This land marks a place where two nations fought to live. Those who failed to claim the land left a curse behind. That is why it remains desolate to this day, why so much danger and evil have befallen it. The new owners should give up their plans and go back to where they came from. Find a new place to build their business. Madrona Grove is not it."

"I see," Gabe said, though wariness in his eyes indicated otherwise. "Unfortunately, I doubt Matt and Vanessa Vanguard will be willing to heed your warning. They've invested a lot into this land. And so has *Restaurant Restarts*. But thank you for your time, Ms. Snowbird. Cut!"

Garth groaned in frustration. "Seriously, Gabe?"

"This conversation was going nowhere," the host snapped, then backed away from Georgine. "Maybe you should leave now. I don't like the way you're looking at me."

"It's not me you should fear," Georgine said in her solemn way.

"All right, that's it. Get me away from this woman." With a final snort of disgust, Gabe stormed off toward the trailers.

As he was passing the kitchen trailer, a petite woman with golden blonde hair and a pert nose stepped out of it and collided with the host. Instead of apologizing, Gabe brushed her aside—a little too forcefully in Kaylee's opinion. Bear seemed to agree, since he issued a bark of rebuke.

"Watch where you're going," Gabe growled, then continued to the next trailer. A moment later, the metal door slammed behind him.

Recognizing the woman, Kaylee started toward her. "Are you all right, Vanessa?"

But Vanessa Vanguard didn't notice Kaylee. Instead, the shock and disdain on her face were aimed at a lean, muscular man with curly brown hair striding toward her—her husband, Matt, who had been milling around near the barn during filming. The married couple seemed to communicate with only facial expressions instead of words, and they soon disappeared back into the kitchen trailer.

"What was all that about?" Jessica asked, appearing at Kaylee's side. "Did I hear Georgine say something about a curse?"

Considering Jessica's penchant for conspiracy theories, Kaylee wasn't surprised that the baker had latched on to that particular part of the interview. It was certainly concerning, but as Kaylee caught sight of Reese staring hard at Gabe's trailer, she couldn't help but feel as if there was more than one kind of trouble haunting the set of *Restaurant Restarts*.

Claiming that they were "losing good light," though it was only midafternoon, Garth and Sawyer had canceled the rest of filming Sunday, sending all the volunteers and lookie-loos home for the day. Since the Petal Pushers hadn't finished their planting, Kaylee returned to the farm a few days later to get their remaining seedlings in the ground so they'd take root at a similar pace to the rest of the garden.

As she pulled into the parking area at Madrona Grove, she saw a familiar white van already there. Holly Sampson, a local organic gardener, stood behind the vehicle, retrieving a large basket of produce from the cargo area. When she caught sight of Kaylee, she smiled and waved.

"I didn't realize you'd be here today," Holly said as Kaylee climbed out of her Ford Escape and led Bear over to the van. Holly gave Kaylee a hug, then stooped to pet Bear, and he leaned happily into her hand. "I would have brought some treats for my buddy here."

"A little attention is plenty of treat for him," Kaylee replied. She saw two bushel baskets overflowing with colorful vegetables in the back of the van. "Although it looks like you brought plenty of other stuff today. Making a delivery?"

Holly lowered her voice. "Yes, but it's hush-hush. The farm's plants obviously won't be producing soon enough for filming, so they're sourcing produce from me for the shoot. Vanessa ordered a list of things she's growing here so it'll match up with their footage of the garden."

"That makes sense." Bear's leash in one hand, Kaylee reached for the handle of a basket with her other. "I'll help you carry them in before I get to work on the garden."

"Thanks, Kaylee." Holly grabbed the other basket and closed the trunk door, then the women started toward the kitchen trailer. "Do you think people will find out the farm didn't actually grow the food being shown on camera?"

"I doubt it. Everything seems to be a facade, and no one has caught on yet." Kaylee pointed to the mostly-repaired barn roof.

"They had Reese leave a small section of the roof unfinished so Gabe could do it on camera."

Holly's mouth dropped open. "Are you serious?"

"All this time, I thought the host was the carpenter." Kaylee pulled a face. "Turns out he just plays one on TV."

They reached the kitchen trailer, which would serve as Vanessa's cooking station until Reese and his crew completed her new, state-of-the-art kitchen at the back of the barn. Before Kaylee could knock on the metal door, however, it opened and Matt stomped out. He mumbled "hey" as he passed, but otherwise didn't acknowledge them.

Kaylee caught the door before it slammed behind Matt. She poked her head inside the cramped trailer, which was packed with kitchen appliances and smelled enticingly like sautéed garlic and fresh bread. Vanessa stood with her back against the refrigerator, her arms crossed in front of her chest and a scowl on her face. The frown lessened when she noticed Kaylee and Holly.

"Should we come back later?" Kaylee asked warily, though Bear was already straining at his leash to enter the trailer.

Vanessa waved her hand dismissively. "Don't pay any attention to Matt."

"Is everything okay?" Holly set her basket of vegetables on the counter beside two large serving platters topped with delicious-looking entrees. "He seemed upset."

"That's just because I told him he's got to clean up this mess he's gotten us into," Vanessa replied tartly.

"Mess?" Kaylee's brow furrowed. "Do you mean the show?"

Vanessa nodded sharply. "I'm the one who's got more right to be upset. That Gabe Forester is a real piece of work. We filmed him testing a few of my new dishes this morning, and he practically spit the food out. Told me it was garbage."

"How terrible," Kaylee said sympathetically as she handed

Vanessa the other basket of vegetables. She reeled in Bear's leash and reached down to pick him up, knowing he shouldn't be wandering free in a commercial kitchen, even if it was somewhat makeshift.

"I told Sawyer that there's no way I'm getting back on camera with that rat," Vanessa continued. "Gabe can hurl his insults at thin air from now on."

"Do you think it's all part of the show?" Holly asked. "Maybe he's supposed to tear you down at first, then *Restaurant Restarts* 'teaches' you how to create a better menu."

"It wouldn't be very kind of the showrunners to set you up like that, though," Kaylee said. "They should have at least warned you if that's the case."

"I should have been warned about a lot of things," Vanessa murmured, then started unloading the baskets into the sink. Her face brightened. "These veggies are gorgeous, Holly."

"I'm glad you're pleased," Holly said, her face brightening. Kaylee knew she cared about the plants in her greenhouse as if they were pets.

"Even the onions look like I could just take a big bite out of them." Vanessa appeared thoughtful for a moment, then her eyes lit up. "I know exactly what to make next. Maybe that know-it-all out there will like my Veggie Vigor juice."

"That sounds healthy," Kaylee said, absentmindedly rubbing Bear behind the ears.

Vanessa laughed. "It is, but it's also delicious. People line up for it in front of the trendy restaurant I work at in L.A." Her mirth faded in an instant. "Or I should say *worked* at before I packed up and moved here like an idiot. What a disaster. What was Matt thinking?" She shook her head in disbelief, then turned the faucet on to wash the vegetables.

"I take it moving here wasn't your idea," Kaylee said gently.

The chef shrugged as she washed a beefsteak tomato. "Don't get me wrong, I've always wanted to live on Orcas Island. And opening a farm to table restaurant is a dream that Matt and I have always shared, since it suits his interest in farming and my passion for cooking. But I'm a private person, and Matt didn't tell me he applied for the television show. It wasn't my idea, and yet I'm the one taking the criticism that know-it-all host flings at me."

"You're right, it doesn't sound fair," Holly agreed.

Vanessa set the tomato aside and picked up a green pepper. "But Matt will fix it. He promised to make all this go away so we can handle the renovation our own way. Some things he can't fix, but this he can."

Vanessa grew quiet as she vigorously scrubbed the dirt from a carrot. Kaylee thought she heard her sniffing back tears.

"Do you want any help?" Holly asked.

Vanessa sniffed again and shook her head. "No thanks. These awesome veggies are all I need." She forced a smile and joked, "If this juice doesn't shut him up, there's no hope for me."

After a round of goodbyes, Kaylee and Holly left the trailer, and Kaylee set Bear down. He snuffled at the ground, leading the women away from the trailer toward the barn.

"How do you suppose Matt plans to make all this go away?"

Kaylee thought of all the work so many islanders had already done, herself included, to make the Madrona Grove renovation a success. Many had volunteered for small projects, as the Petal Pushers had done in planting the garden, but others were expecting payment for their time. Reese and his crew had put in countless hours rehabbing the property, and Jessica and Kaylee had been contracted to provide services for the upcoming wedding. If filming was shut down and the wedding was canceled, would they still be compensated? "I don't know how Matt can make it go away, but if he does, I hope it won't be at a great cost to the people who've been contributing their time and energy for weeks."

"It would be best if all this went away, no matter the cost." At the sound of an unexpected voice, Kaylee whipped around to find Georgine Snowbird standing in the shadow of a trailer, holding her little leather pouch again.

"Ms. Snowbird," Kaylee said. "I didn't expect to see you here again."

"No one has heeded my warning," the older woman replied. "This circus needs to go away. The spirits are not happy. They will have the last word." Georgine slipped further into the shadows and disappeared behind the trailer.

"What was that all about?" Holly asked, her eyes wide.

Kaylee quickly told her friend about Madrona Grove's history, the alleged curse on the property, and Georgine's warning about wrathful spirits.

Holly grimaced. "Why would she want to frighten people like that?"

Kaylee shrugged, unable to shake a feeling that Georgine actually meant well, despite her tactics. "Maybe she knows something we don't."

"Maybe." Holly glanced around. "Hey, do you think I can stay and watch for a while? I've never seen a TV show filmed before."

Kaylee nodded. "People from town pop by all the time. As long as we stay off camera and keep our voices down, we should be okay." After a cursory scan of their surroundings, she said, "It doesn't look like they're filming now. Do you want a tour of the farm?"

Holly agreed quickly, so Kaylee led her friend through the barn, where Reese and his small crew were putting up walls to section off the restaurant's kitchen. She didn't want to interrupt his work, so she just waved and smiled, receiving the same in return, then guided Holly out to the large garden. After discussing the crops for a few minutes, they continued past the free-range chicken coop to a lush, green pasture where a small herd of cows grazed—a far cry from the sad patch of dirt Gabe had chastised on film, which was actually going to be the site of the new cowshed being built that week. Kaylee mentioned this untruth to Holly, who rolled her eyes.

Eventually, they ended up back near the front of the barn, where the crew had set up a camera aimed at a table containing dishes of food. Nearby, Suzy was touching up Gabe's makeup, and Garth, Sawyer, and Nino were clustered behind the camera. Matt leaned back against the barn, his arms crossed.

"Let's try this again, Gabe," Garth called as Kaylee and Holly edged closer for a better view. "On your mark, please."

Somewhat to Kaylee's surprise, Gabe did as instructed without comment and quickly plastered on a camera-ready smile. After a cue from Garth, he addressed the camera. "Today I'll be taste testing some recipes Vanessa prepared and offering her some friendly criticism to help her take her menu from ho-hum to 'holy cow!'" Gabe's face exploded into an animated expression as he said the last words—his catchphrase, if Kaylee remembered correctly.

The camera continued rolling as Gabe picked up a fork. "This first is a beet salad with arugula and fennel, all grown right here at Madrona Grove. It's topped with fresh mozzarella made with milk from cows on the farm." He took a small bite, grimaced, and swallowed quickly. "Terrible mix of flavors. And the arugula is a soggy disaster."

"He certainly isn't mincing words, is he?" Holly murmured to Kaylee. "Poor Vanessa."

Still frowning, Gabe grabbed for a water glass. After a swift chug, he continued with the next two dishes, giving similar negative reactions to them. Finally, he spit his last bite into a napkin. "I can't keep up this charade for you folks at home. This food is absolutely inedible. That disgusting pepper quiche was mush—and did that incompetent woman even wash the beets before she put them in that awful salad?"

Kaylee recoiled from the venom Gabe was spewing, and she would have stepped up to defend Vanessa in a heartbeat if her husband hadn't done it first.

Matt stormed forward into the camera's line of sight. "Vanessa is a fine chef," he snarled at Gabe. "You haven't given her a chance. All you do is criticize, trying to get her riled up. Well, I can get riled up too. We don't need you."

Gabe flicked a glance at the camera, then squared his shoulders. "That's where you're wrong, Matt. You do need me. You need a miracle if you think you will make it in the restaurant business. But don't worry. Your miracle is here, and I plan to take your little half-baked pipe dream and make it a great success. The first step is making sure you have a great product to sell, or you'll be serving ghosts at empty tables."

His fist clenched, Matt appeared ready to take a swing at the host, but the moment was interrupted by the director calling "Cut!" Garth jumped up from his chair. "That was great, guys. Matt, I loved how you came roaring in to stand up for your wife. So romantic. The viewers will love it. But please, check with us in the future. We only have so much daylight to work with."

Matt appeared aghast at the implication that he was putting on a show. "I meant what I said."

Sawyer stepped in. "Of course you did. You meant every word. You would do anything for your wife. And you already have—you're making her dream of owning a farm to table restaurant a reality, and you've asked us to make it world-class, which is what we're trying to do. When we're done here, your reservations will be booked a year in advance."

"I certainly hope so." Matt's gaze went to the table, and he pointed to a tall glass of red liquid with a skewer of vegetables laid across the top. "You didn't try Vanessa's Veggie Vigor juice yet, Gabe. Why don't you use it to wash down all that 'inedible' food?"

"Yes, that's a great idea," Sawyer agreed. "It's her signature recipe, after all."

"Fine." Gabe grabbed the glass. "Let's go. It's past my break time."

"We'll try to get it in one take," Garth said. "Places!"

Gabe's charm returned as soon as cameras were rolling, and Kaylee fought back a sense of disquiet over the man's mercurial shifts.

Reading off the teleprompter, Gabe said, "In addition to the charm of dining next to the garden that grew your dinner, Matt and Vanessa's restaurant also focuses on health-conscious offerings, such as this Veggie Vigor juice, Vanessa's signature recipe. It contains a whole day's nutrients, and I'm told it also pairs well with steak." With a wink at the camera, he removed the long toothpick of veggies and bit a pearl onion off the end. He chewed it quickly, then took a long drink of the vegetable juice and swallowed hard. "Cut!" he yelled.

"Gabe—" Garth began, but the host interrupted him.

"This is disgusting." Gabe dumped the rest of the drink in the grass with a flourish. "No one will ever eat at this travesty of a restaurant if this is what you think qualifies as food." He slammed the glass back on the table with a loud *thud*. "I'll be in my trailer for when you're all serious about making something of this place. Until then, don't bother me."

"You don't call the shots," Garth said, jumping up from

his chair. "Be back in one hour. We still have the orchard to shoot at sunset."

If Gabe heard, he didn't respond as he stomped off to his trailer. Noticing that none of the other crew members seemed particularly bothered by the scene that had just played out, Kaylee wondered if the spectacle had been real. She didn't know where the show's Hollywood magic started or ended. "Is this typical for a reality television set?" she wondered out loud.

The cameraman, Nino, glanced up from the playback monitor at her question. He squinted at Kaylee for a moment, clearly trying to figure out how he knew her. "Wait, don't tell me. The plant lady, right?"

"Yes, Kaylee Bleu. And this is Holly Sampson, the produce supplier." After Nino nodded hello to Holly, Kaylee tilted her head and said, "I'm just trying to figure out what's real and what's not around here. What's true and what's made up for the camera."

"We have a saying in television, plant lady: If it didn't happen on camera, then it didn't happen." Nino smirked, then returned his focus to the monitor.

Kaylee got the picture. The truth was only what was filmed. But what if that wasn't the real truth?

3

After Holly left, Kaylee returned to the garden to finish planting the seedlings. She looped Bear's leash over a fence post so that he could sit on the grass to watch her and the other goings-on at the farm. Once the planting was completed, she dragged a hose from the barn over to the garden and watered everything. As she was coiling the hose back up on the rack attached to the barn, Garth emerged from the building at a purposeful pace.

"Where's Gabe?" he bellowed. "We're all set up to film by the orchard, and it'd be nice to do it before midnight."

Suzy, who had been lingering around her makeup station, shrugged. "He hasn't come out of his trailer, and I've been waiting for him," she said, her tone impatient. "I need time to work the miracles you people expect."

"Why didn't you knock on his door?" Garth stomped up to Gabe's trailer and rapped on the metal door. "Let's go, Gabe! We don't have all day. It's almost sunset."

Several moments went by with no response. Garth banged harder, the sound of clanging metal louder this time. The door swung wide.

"I'm coming," Gabe grumbled and stepped out. "Why do you have to be so loud? My head is killing me." He stumbled a bit, but Sawyer grabbed hold of his arm to steady him.

"What's the matter with you?" the director asked. "Are you sick? Great. That's just what we need right now."

"You know what they say," Gabe mumbled. "The show must go on." He rubbed his forehead, which was beaded with sweat despite the mild May weather. In spite of the tan and the makeup he wore from earlier, his face still held a sickly pallor.

"I didn't realize you were still here," Reese said as he joined Kaylee. "Lucky me." He leaned in and kissed her cheek, but Kaylee was too focused on Gabe to respond. "Is everything all right?"

Kaylee snapped out of her thoughts and smiled at Reese. "I'm sorry. I'm just a little worried about Gabe."

Reese studied the host as he shuffled by them on his way to the shooting location. "He does seem rather pasty," Reese said. "And a bit disorderly."

Gabe trudged to his mark. Suzy rushed over and doused him with powder, but that only made his complexion worse.

Suddenly, Gabe cried out and started brushing his legs forcefully. "Something bit me!"

Crew members flocked around Gabe, but soon they were all shaking their heads, confused expressions on their faces. Georgine Snowbird emerged from a group of bystanders who had gathered around the cameras.

"The land is cursed, just as I told you," Georgine announced in a loud but solemn voice. Nino swung the closest camera around to capture Georgine as she continued addressing the crew. "Now you will each pay the price for your foolish presence." She pointed to Gabe. "It starts with this man, but who will be next?"

"That's enough, Ms. Snowbird," Garth said from his position behind the camera. "I have to ask you to leave the set."

Georgine stared at him for a moment, then nodded once and walked away.

"Somebody round up Matt," Garth called. "It's time for his interview."

The crew continued with business as usual, despite Gabe still appearing unsteady on his feet as he braced himself against a fence post while Suzy continued to touch up his makeup.

Kaylee shook her head. *Apparently the show really does go on, no matter what.*

"Does Bear need a walk?" Reese asked, breaking into Kaylee's thoughts. "I could use a break with my favorite girl and my favorite dog."

"I'm sure he wouldn't mind a visit to the cows," she answered. "And I wouldn't mind your company."

After retrieving Bear from his tethered spot in the garden, they walked toward the cow pasture, the little dog happily snuffling the ground every few feet along the way.

"How could anybody say this beautiful land is cursed?" Reese asked, gesturing to the picturesque surroundings.

"I don't know what to believe," Kaylee said. "I doubt the land is cursed, though Georgine certainly seems to think so. I can't help but wonder if this is all a ploy for television ratings. I honestly can't tell what's real."

"Unfortunately, in my experience, Gabe isn't always dialed into reality." Reese rested his forearms on the pasture's white fence. "Even twenty years ago, he lived in his own egocentric world."

Kaylee studied Reese's profile for a moment. "How did you two become friends? You're so different. I admit I can't really picture you as close pals."

Reese laughed. "We lived in the same dorm in college. I guess you could say we bonded over some shared experiences." His face darkened.

Kaylee raised an eyebrow. "What is it?"

"Nothing, really. It's just . . . I'm surprised he's been so friendly toward me."

Kaylee nearly laughed. "Well you're one of the only people he's been friendly to around here."

Reese smiled faintly, but the expression disappeared quickly. "The last time we ran into each other in L.A., he wasn't happy to see me. As it turned out, I was dating his ex-girlfriend. He didn't react well to seeing me with Nicole."

"Is that what he meant the other day when he mentioned bygones?" Kaylee asked. She wasn't prone to jealousy, but she was only human, and any reference to Reese's mysterious former fiancée piqued her interest. He almost never mentioned his ex, and Kaylee couldn't help but be curious about the woman who'd stolen his heart and then trampled it mercilessly.

Reese shook his head, clearing the darkness from his features. "I don't want you to give it another thought. It's ancient history."

One of the production assistants hurried over to the pasture fence and waved her arms at Kaylee and Reese. "You've got to move," the young woman hissed without preamble. "Gabe and Matt are doing a walking interview about the orchard, and they're heading this way any second." She cast a suspicious gaze at Bear. "And keep that dog quiet."

Bear hadn't once interrupted filming with a bark, but Kaylee didn't waste time arguing about that. Instead, she scooped up her dog, and then she and Reese hustled into the barn just as Gabe and Matt came around the side of the building, Nino close on their heels with a handheld camera and Garth following at a short distance. The TV host stopped abruptly and doubled over, placing one hand on his knee and swiping at his sweating forehead with his other arm.

"Gabe really doesn't look well," Kaylee said quietly to Reese as they paused inside the doorway to watch.

Before Reese could respond, Gabe righted himself and gazed directly into the barn. "There's my old b-buddy," Gabe said unevenly as he walked over to them. "Don't you go running away from me again, Reese. I want the w-world to meet the guy who s-stole my girl." He eyed Kaylee and smirked. "Maybe I'll have to return the favor."

Reese shifted so that he stood in front of Kaylee, shielding her from Gabe—though not from Nino, who roved freely with his bulky camera on his shoulder. Garth stood in the shadows, his face barely visible.

"Surely your viewers would rather you focus on the farm, Gabe," Reese responded calmly. "Maybe you should move on to another topic more appropriate for the show. Leave the past in the past. I certainly did when I came to live on Orcas Island."

Gabe stumbled as he closed in, and Reese caught the host by the upper arm to steady him.

"You're right, Reese," Gabe said through clenched teeth. "I should leave the past in the past. Start over just like you. This show is getting old."

Kaylee glanced at Garth, whose eyes narrowed at Gabe's words.

"Don't be too hasty. You've done well for yourself." Reese let go of Gabe and stepped back. "How about we take a look at the kitchen going in? I'll give you an update on the progress made today."

"You hear that, Snowbird lady?" Gabe yelled over his shoulder, though Georgine was nowhere to be seen. "Progress has been made here. I guess you were wrong about your curses."

Garth stormed over from the shadows. "That's enough, Gabe. You're obviously sick or looking for a fight. Go to the kitchen trailer to get some water and cool off. We're done for the day." He shook his head and left the barn, muttering, "What a waste."

Gabe stumbled toward the barn door that led to the trailers. Reese and Kaylee exchanged glances, then followed the host to the exit.

"Here, let me help you," Reese said, grasping Gabe's arm.

Gabe shook him off almost violently. "Don't need help from *you*," he sneered, then lurched toward Vanessa's trailer. He nearly fell when he reached the door, but he caught himself and soon disappeared inside.

"I think that's my cue to leave," Kaylee said, setting Bear on the ground.

Reese glanced over his shoulder toward the kitchen in the barn. "I have a few things to wrap up here, but do you want to grab a bite to eat later?"

Kaylee smiled broadly at the idea of spending her evening with him, which hadn't happened much recently. "Why don't you come over to Wildflower Cottage? It's a nice evening. We can grill."

"That sounds perfect," Reese said. "I'll bring the—"

An ear-piercing shriek ripped through the air, the sound sending a flock of birds scattering from the orchard. A moment later, a second shrill scream rang out.

"It's coming from the trailers," Kaylee said as she swept Bear into her arms and started running in that direction.

"Who do you think is screaming?" Reese asked as he jogged beside her.

Kaylee had no answer. They reached the row of trailers at the same time as several other concerned crew members. Kaylee glanced down the line of small structures toward the kitchen trailer. Nino was just disappearing around the back of the building, his camera on his shoulder.

"This way." Kaylee grabbed hold of Reese's hand and hurried toward the cameraman.

Just as they reached the kitchen trailer, Georgine emerged from it, her face drained of all color and eyes widened with fear. Her mouth moved frantically but no sound came out. Finally, a few brutal words escaped her lips. "Mr. Forester . . . is dead!"

4

The crowd erupted with shock at the revelation, and most of the bystanders moved closer to the kitchen trailer. Nino reappeared around the other side of the trailer, his camera still on his shoulder with the red light on its front glowing. He was recording the whole thing.

Kaylee started to approach Georgine, who was wringing her hands and mumbling incoherently in distress, but she stopped short when she noticed Nino filming the herbalist. Not wanting to be on camera, she stayed where she was and watched the cameraman. The lens seemed to be focused on Georgine's empty hands. *Where did her satchel of herbs go? Did she drop it inside?*

Deciding that comforting Georgine and maybe learning what she knew about Gabe's death was more important than her discomfort at being filmed, Kaylee finally approached the frightened older woman. But before she could ask anything, the herbalist cried out, "I warned him to leave before it was too late! Why didn't he listen to me?"

"Are you sure he's dead?" Kaylee asked gently, laying a hand on Georgine's shoulder. Although Georgine nodded, Kaylee sensed hesitation from her. She looked to Reese. "We need to check on him."

"Kaylee, I—" Reese didn't get a chance to finish before Kaylee had opened the metal trailer door and stepped inside. "At least let me take Bear."

Kaylee did a double take, feeling a rush of guilt that she'd been about to carry her beloved dog inside. She quickly handed him off to Reese with an appreciative smile. "Thank you."

Inside the trailer, the first thing Kaylee spotted was Gabe's feet, the soles of his expensive leather shoes scuffed and dirty from walking around on the farm. He lay facedown, and his black hair now appeared mussed and out of place for the first time since he'd arrived on the island. Kaylee slowly approached him, careful not to touch anything as she studied him. His hands were at his sides, one fisted tight and partially obscured by his body, the other with fingers slightly curved.

She leaned down and placed her fingers at his neck.

No pulse.

Kaylee kept her fingers there a little longer, hoping she was wrong . . . but she wasn't.

"He's dead," she said quietly, though the trailer was empty. Vanessa was gone, although she'd left a small pile of produce on the counter beside a large cooking knife. Recoiling at the sight of the gleaming blade, Kaylee quickly scanned Gabe's body for signs that he'd been attacked by one of the other knives in the set. There was no blood visible on Gabe's crisp blue shirt, nor was any pooling on the floor beneath his body. In fact, the trailer looked the same as it had a few hours earlier when Kaylee and Holly had chatted with Vanessa.

Kaylee became aware of a commotion outside the trailer, and she heard Sawyer's usual take-charge tone say, "Let us by." A moment later, he and Garth pushed their way into the cramped trailer, crowding Kaylee up against the refrigerator.

"What are you doing in here, Katie?" Sawyer demanded.

"It's Kaylee," she corrected. "And I am here to help."

"We don't need your help," Sawyer said, but his bravado faltered when he spotted Gabe's body.

Garth's face took on a grim countenance as well, but he stood tall. "You shouldn't be in here."

"None of us should," Kaylee replied. "We don't want to disrupt the crime scene."

"Crime scene?" Sawyer yelped.

"Potential crime scene," Kaylee amended. "Gabe is dead, and we don't know why. Everything in here should remain untouched until the sheriff's department arrives."

"I already called the authorities," Garth said. "They're on their way."

As if on cue, Kaylee heard the sound of sirens in the distance. "Then let's get out of the trailer. Make sure nobody goes in unless they're from the sheriff's department."

Garth and Sawyer exited the building first, followed by Kaylee, who made her way back to Reese's side. She rubbed Bear's head, as much to greet him as to comfort herself.

"He's dead," she murmured to Reese.

"What happened?" Reese asked.

Kaylee shook her head. "I don't know. There's no blood."

"He was acting strangely. He could have been sick." Reese grew visibly uncomfortable as Nino edged closer to them, his ever-present camera at the ready.

By silent agreement, Kaylee and Reese stopped discussing the matter as Sawyer held up his hands to quiet the questions being shouted from the crowd.

"It brings me great sadness to announce that our very own Gabe Forester has passed away," Sawyer announced. "He was a one-of-a-kind personality, dedicated to his craft and beloved by everyone who had the pleasure of his company."

Standing nearby, Suzy the makeup artist issued a derisive snort. "As if," she murmured just loud enough for Kaylee to hear.

"While we wait for the authorities to handle this delicate matter, I must ask that all of you give this area a wide berth," Sawyer continued. "But don't leave the property. I'm sure they'll want to talk to everyone, especially anybody Gabe might have encountered in the kitchen trailer—likely starting with the chef herself." Sawyer's gaze swept the crowd. "Has anyone seen Vanessa, by the way?"

Matt stepped to the front of the group. "She needed a break from this circus, so she took a walk in the orchard. She has nothing to do with this."

"That remains for the police to determine, I'm afraid." Sawyer squinted toward the road leading into the farm. "And here they are now."

A series of sheriff's department cruisers sped down the dirt lane, their lights flashing. Trailing them was an ambulance, and Kaylee felt a surge of sadness that the EMTs' assistance would be futile. Gabe had obviously been a complicated man, but he certainly hadn't deserved to suffer an untimely death.

The vehicles soon parked near the trailers. Sheriff Eddie Maddox climbed out of the first car, placed his hat on top of his gray-speckled black hair, and strode confidently toward the crowd. "Who's in charge here?" he asked.

Sawyer stepped forward. "I'm Sawyer Hawkins, the creator and producer of *Restaurant Restarts*."

"Could you tell me what happened?" Sheriff Maddox scanned the group of bystanders. "I'd appreciate if you all could give us some space. Just don't go far."

As the crowd dispersed, Sawyer, Garth, and Eddie clustered to one side, joined a few moments later by Deputies Nick Durham, Robyn Garcia, and Alan Brooks. Kaylee couldn't hear what was said, but she did notice Sawyer pointing at her at least once during the discussion.

After some words and a final nod from the sheriff, the group broke apart, and Eddie approached Kaylee and Reese, who were lingering beside the trailer. "I hear you were first on the scene in there, aside from Ms. Snowbird," he said. "Can't say I'm surprised."

Considering her history of working with the Orcas Island Sheriff's Department—both as a forensic botanist and in other, less official ways—Kaylee found the sheriff's teasing to be endearing. He was a kindhearted, fair lawman, and she knew that he appreciated her contributions. "At least you always know where to find me," she said.

Amusement briefly flitted across the sheriff's face, then he turned serious. "What can you tell me about what I'm going to see in there?"

"He's lying on the floor, but there are no signs of a struggle or blood." Kaylee pursed her lips. "Gabe was acting strange earlier. He was sweating, disoriented, and stuttering a bit."

"Interesting." Eddie opened the trailer door. "Thanks, Kaylee. I'll be in touch if I need anything else." He disappeared inside.

Reese placed a hand on Kaylee's shoulder and squeezed gently. "So what now?"

Kaylee leaned into Reese and accepted a friendly lick from Bear as she rubbed her dog's ears. "It depends on what they determine to be the cause of death."

"Do you think Gabe was sick?" Reese asked, setting a squirming Bear on the ground so the dachshund could investigate nearby smells. "He just flew in a few days ago. Do you know where he was before? If he was somewhere exotic, he could have picked up a strange disease of some sort."

"Or it could have been poison." Kaylee's blood went icy at the realization. "The symptoms came on so suddenly—"

"Kaylee, can you come in here for a moment?" The sheriff had reappeared at the trailer door.

Kaylee frowned, wondering what more Eddie might need from her. She entered the trailer and asked, "What is it, Sheriff?"

Eddie indicated a leather pouch barely visible in Gabe's clenched fist. "You wouldn't happen to know anything about this, would you?"

Kaylee hadn't noticed it before, but she instantly recognized the pouch as Georgine's, and she recoiled slightly. Gabe must have been alive when Georgine was inside the trailer with him for it to be in his hand. Had she given him the pouch? Had he taken it from her?

"Ms. Snowbird said it holds lavender for calming her nerves," Kaylee said.

"So it belongs to Georgine Snowbird?"

"She's the one who alerted us to Gabe's death."

"That's what Mr. Hawkins told us." The sheriff's brow furrowed. "Isn't she a Lummi herbalist? What was she doing on the set of a reality television show?"

"She lives next door, and she was invited to be interviewed by Gabe about the history of the land," Kaylee explained. She hesitated, wondering if she should tell the sheriff everything Georgine had said. Then she realized that if she didn't tell him, someone else certainly would. "Her interview didn't go as Gabe expected, though. She said that two tribes had fought over the land centuries ago, and Madrona Grove is cursed. When Gabe was stumbling around earlier, she said that he was the first to pay the price."

"Well, Kaylee," Eddie said, "It seems you've led me to another case that's far more complicated than it first appeared." He reached for his radio. "Durham, please come inside the trailer."

A moment later, the handsome and flirtatious Deputy Nick Durham arrived in the trailer. He nodded a greeting to Kaylee, his expression unsurprised at her presence, then asked, "What do you need, Sheriff?"

"When Giles gets here, I want you to process every inch of this trailer while he examines the body," Eddie answered, referring to local coroner Giles Akin. "While you do that, I believe I need to have a chat with Ms. Snowbird."

"Yes sir," Nick said. "Ms. Snowbird is outside."

"Good." Eddie nodded and started for the door, which Kaylee took as her cue to leave as well.

Nick moved aside to let them pass, but he held up a hand. "You should know the camera guy is filming right now."

"What for? The host is dead. The show's over. These reality crews will amp up any bit of drama they can find. And if they can't find it, they'll invent it." Sheriff Maddox shook his head and exited the trailer with Kaylee.

Outside, Kaylee scanned the farm for Reese, who was no longer close to the trailer. She spotted him across the barnyard, leading a frolicking Bear on a walk around the grounds. She smiled, appreciating the initiative he'd taken to occupy the little dog, who was likely growing antsy. She waved, and Reese held up a finger to indicate that he and Bear would return momentarily.

The sheriff walked a few yards farther to Georgine, who sat on a weathered picnic table. From where she waited, Kaylee could hear their conversation clearly.

"Ms. Snowbird, could you please tell me why the deceased has your medicine pouch clenched in his fist?" Eddie asked.

"He reached for me as he fell." Georgine's voice was slow and deep. "I was too far away, and all he was able to grab was my bag. I didn't even realize I'd let it go. Once I figured out he was dead, I started screaming and ran out of the trailer."

"Why were you in there with him?" Sheriff Maddox asked.

"I could tell he was getting sicker. He needed to leave before it was too late. But my warnings were not heeded." Georgine bowed her head.

Out of the corner of her eye, Kaylee caught a flash of movement as Nino and his camera maneuvered for a better angle on the sheriff's conversation with Georgine. Kaylee was about to walk over and tell him he ought to have more respect for the fact that Gabe was dead, but she didn't get a chance.

Someone gripped Kaylee's arm, startling her. Vanessa stood beside her, her eyes red and puffy as if she'd been crying. "Kaylee, I . . ."

"Are you okay?" Kaylee quickly wrapped her new friend in a reassuring hug, then nodded a greeting to Matt, who stood just behind his wife. "This is all so terrible."

"I can't believe it happened in my trailer." Vanessa sobbed into Kaylee's shoulder.

"I'm just glad you weren't in there, honey," Matt said.

"Where were you?" Kaylee asked Vanessa.

"In the orchard. After hearing what that man had to say about my food, I went for a walk past the cow pasture to clear my head, to get away from all this insanity." Vanessa's breath hitched. "But maybe if I'd been there, Gabe wouldn't be . . ."

The chef dissolved into tears once more, and Kaylee patted her back sympathetically. Finally, Vanessa broke away from Kaylee and returned to Matt's side. He put a protective arm around her and held her close, his own face stoic or shell-shocked—Kaylee couldn't tell which.

Kaylee eyed Nino, who had edged closer to the Vanguards.

"You'd think I'd be glad," Vanessa said before Kaylee could send her a warning look. "I suppose part of me is. I mean, all of this chaos will go away, and Matt and I can focus on getting the farm and restaurant prepared at our own pace so we can open when *we* are ready. I can't say for sure when that will be, but—"

"Well, I can," Sawyer broke in tartly. "You talk like we're closing up shop and slinking off with our tail between our legs."

Matt gazed at the man in confusion. "Aren't you? Your host is dead. How can you continue the show?"

Sawyer crossed his arms. "This is my show, and I'll come up with a way to see it through. One way or another."

Vanessa smiled sweetly at the producer. "That's not necessary. We appreciate the offer, but we'll take it from here."

Sawyer shook his head. "I think you've forgotten you signed a contract."

Vanessa's smile evaporated. She lifted her chin and leveled her shoulders. "I didn't sign anything."

"Well your husband did," Sawyer said smugly. "Didn't take much convincing to get him on board with the show either."

Resentment flashed in Vanessa's eyes. "Yes, well, he doesn't value his privacy nearly as much as I do."

Matt sighed, the sound a mixture of remorse and frustration. "I thought I was doing something good, Vanessa. That this land and farm would make you happy. You've been so down ever since—"

Vanessa raised a hand to stop him from saying more. "You made a huge decision without consulting me. If you thought this . . . this . . . *fiasco* would help me, you thought wrong. It's been the opposite of helpful from day one. I've been the one taking Gabe's vitriol since he arrived. Not you. He was mean and judgmental, and he almost seemed to enjoy humiliating me. I'm sorry he's dead, but I'm not sorry the show is over." She fixed her gaze on Sawyer. "And it *is* over."

"Wrong. I say when it's over." Sawyer reached into his pocket and retrieved a folded packet of papers. "This is a copy of the contract. I kept it on hand, just in case Matt 'lost' his." The producer opened the packet and pointed to something on the page. Nino and his camera closed in. "This number is what you will owe us if you break the contract. Plus our legal fees, of course."

Matt closed his eyes and rubbed his forehead.

"This is all your fault," Vanessa hissed at her husband, her glare searing. "This circus, Gabe's death—it's all your fault."

As Vanessa stormed away toward the cows, Nino zoomed in on Matt's crumpled face. "I was only trying to fix everything," he pleaded to his wife's back as he started to run after her. "Vanessa, wait!"

Sheriff Maddox, who had apparently been listening, cleared his throat with authority. "This show may be contracted to continue, but a man is dead, and until I know the cause, I will need to treat this incident as foul play."

"Are you ordering us not to film?" Sawyer's chest puffed up as if he was readying for a fight.

"Ordering you?" Eddie repeated. "No, Mr. Hawkins, I'm not. I am going to caution you to tread lightly here, however. I don't take kindly to people stirring up trouble on my island."

Sawyer smiled. "Certainly, Sheriff. Though I'm sure you can understand where I'm coming from. I've got a whole lot of people counting on paychecks, and they won't get paid if there's no show."

"As long as those people are safe," Sheriff Maddox said.

"Of course." Sawyer placed a hand on his heart. "If Gabe had shared that he wasn't feeling well, I would have made sure he sought medical attention." He glanced toward Georgine, who sat out of earshot at a picnic table, then lowered his voice and said, "That Snowbird woman may have had something to do with getting him sick. Gabe didn't like her at all. In fact, he wanted her off the property. He told me she tried to give him a concoction of herbs to ward off some so-called curse. I would check to see what she has on her."

"Thank you for sharing what you know," Eddie said. "I'll be sure the coroner does a toxicology report."

As Kaylee watched Georgine wring her hands, she thought about how the herbalist had been the last to see Gabe alive and the first to see him dead. And her pouch had been clutched in Gabe's hands. Had there been something in the bag besides lavender?

"Sheriff," she said, stepping up to the two men. "I could test for residue of any other herbs that might have been in the bag previously. She showed me the other day that it was lavender, but perhaps there's been something else in it since."

"Thank you, Kaylee." The sheriff nodded. "Once it's been cataloged, I'll turn the evidence over to you for testing." His gaze rested on the cow pasture, where Vanessa and Matt stood alone by the fence. The two didn't touch, and it was obvious there was a strain in their marriage. "If you'll excuse me, I'd like to speak to the owners."

As Eddie walked away, Sawyer beckoned to his cameraman, who stood nearby. "Tell me, Nino—how much of this did you catch?"

"As much as I could, Boss," Nino replied. "Definitely got some good stuff of the medicine woman going crazy."

"Good man." Sawyer slapped Nino on the shoulder jovially. "Thanks for rolling today. If you hadn't captured what went down, we wouldn't have a show to continue with."

"Just capturing the story you set in motion, Boss."

Kaylee fought a sense of queasiness as she watched the two men congratulating each other mere yards from the trailer where their colleague lay dead. But before she said anything, a welcome, familiar bark broke into her thoughts. She turned to see Reese heading her way with Bear.

"Sorry, we ran into Robyn Garcia and she wanted to ask me some questions," Reese said. "Then I got to talking with some of the crew members. They're pretty freaked out."

"Me too," Kaylee admitted as she bent to give Bear his due. "This whole situation is creepy." *And not just the dead television host.*

"Then let's get out of here." Reese put an arm around her shoulders as she stood, then started leading her toward the parking area.

"See you tomorrow, Reese," Sawyer called. "Bright and early, right?"

Reese frowned, confused, and faced the producer. "You want me to keep working?"

"The sheriff just told you to tread carefully," Kaylee said, unable to stop herself. "You're really going to continue with an unsolved death hanging over your heads?"

"Lots of people are counting on us to complete this project," Sawyer said evenly. "Not to mention the people who might not get paid if it doesn't get finished."

Was that a threat to Reese? Kaylee glanced sharply at Sawyer, but his expression seemed innocent.

"I'll be here," Reese said, his tone shorter than was his usual laid-back manner.

Sawyer clapped his hands together. "Great. And plan to have dinner with me in town tomorrow. I'd like to go over what our next steps will be for the show. You can come too, Katie." He put a hand on the cameraman's back. "Come on, Nino. Let's go watch the playback of what we got today."

When the other men walked away, Kaylee peered into Reese's face. She could sense that something wasn't sitting well with him. "Are you sure you want to keep working on the farm after all that's happened?"

Reese nodded solemnly. "There's rain in the forecast later this week, so I need to get the roof finished. Gabe didn't . . . didn't have a chance to."

Kaylee quickly understood why Reese was upset. "I'm sorry you didn't get to really make amends with him."

Reese sighed. "I know it had been a while since I saw Gabe, but we were close at one time. I should have taken the time to talk to him, to clear the air, but now—"

"Now you feel like things are left undone." Kaylee rubbed

his arm. "But it sounded as though Gabe wanted to make things right with you. And I don't think you would have worked this job if you still held a grudge against him. Right?"

Reese breathed in deeply, then exhaled, his face thoughtful. He offered a subdued smile. "You're right. Thank you for putting things into perspective for me." Reese pulled Kaylee into a hug, then took her hand. They headed to the parking lot, Bear leading the way.

"I wish somebody would put things in perspective for Sawyer." Kaylee glanced back toward the trailer he and Nino had disappeared into to watch their footage. "I can't believe he won't put the shoot on hold."

"Whether they're filming or not, we need to get this farm ready to host a wedding later this month."

Kaylee put a hand to her cheek. She'd nearly forgotten that a local couple was relying on Madrona Grove's renovation to be completed in time to host their nuptials. She frowned. "Do you think Josh and Savannah will still want to get married here after someone died during filming?"

"If they're anything like Sawyer," Reese said as they reached Kaylee's SUV, "they'll probably agree that the show must go on."

As Kaylee put Bear in the car and then climbed into the driver's seat, Georgine's warning about the cursed land floated back to the top of her mind. Sure, the show could go on, despite everything that had happened—but at what cost?

5

With warm temperatures remaining after sunset, the patio at O'Brien's restaurant was still open for Kayiee and Reese's dinner with Sawyer the next night. Kaylee was glad since it meant she could bring Bear along. She wasn't thrilled to be dining with the smug TV producer, but she knew that Reese appreciated her being there with him—and having her four-legged best friend around would add some much needed levity. She'd dressed him in a red-and-white bow tie, and she was just adjusting it when Sawyer strode up to their table with Garth trailing behind.

"Good evening, Reese, Katie," Sawyer said in greeting. He took in the driftwood tables and other seaside decor. "I see why you chose this place. It's certainly got ambiance."

"*Kaylee* and I love coming here," Reese said. Kaylee smiled at him, appreciating the correction.

"Is that barnwood siding?" Garth asked as he sat down across from Kaylee. O'Brien's interior seating was housed in a building designed to resemble an old fishing shack. "You don't think it's too similar to the ambiance at the farm, do you, Sawyer?"

"You might be right. Maybe Reese should repaint the barn at Madrona Grove again," the producer answered breezily. "And the new tables to match. I'm picturing yellow."

Kaylee and Reese exchanged glances. "My crew already painted the barn red, Sawyer," Reese said. "Painting it again, especially a lighter color, will take a lot of time and more money."

Sawyer shrugged. "Well, without Gabe's star power, we've got to find another way to make a splash. If nobody tunes in to the show, nobody will come to the restaurant. If people can get the same ambiance in town, why would they drive all the way out to that farm?"

Kaylee couldn't fathom what the color of the barn and furniture had to do with the restaurant's success. "Isn't Vanessa's food supposed to be what sets their restaurant apart?" Kaylee asked. "O'Brien's is great, but it's pub fare, not farm to table, organic fine dining. If you're worried about them being too similar, don't be."

"Unless a famous TV host dropped dead at this place, I suppose we don't have to be concerned about being too similar," Garth said with false levity. The joke fell flat.

"So have you guys worked together a long time?" Kaylee asked, hoping to ease the awkward moment.

Sawyer laughed. "Garth and I go way back. He's always been my right-hand man. The most reliable guy in Hollywood, not that that's saying much. I get these crazy ideas, and he's the one who figures out how to make them work."

A stiff smile was barely visible behind Garth's bushy beard, but it didn't quite reach his eyes. "Sawyer's a real visionary. I'm lucky to be along for the ride, whether his ideas pan out or not."

"You win some, you lose some. Eh, old pal?" Sawyer slapped Garth on the back, and Kaylee sensed a frisson of tension between the men, but it vanished as quickly as it had appeared. "I'll admit, I thought *Restaurant Restarts* was going to be one of my crazier whims, but it has been a surprising success for me. And it hasn't gotten old. I love the adrenaline rush I get every time something unexpected happens while we're filming."

A server arrived at the table and set down glasses of ice water. "Welcome to O'Brien's," she said. "Our specials are battered fish and chips, and an eight-ounce strip steak with your choice of side. And our soup of the day is clam chowder."

Reese gave her his menu. "Steak for me, please, with a baked potato."

"And the fish for me," Kaylee said, handing over her menu as well.

The waitress shifted her attention to Sawyer and Garth. "How about you guys?"

Sawyer checked his watch. "Maybe just chowder for us. We're kind of pressed for time."

Kaylee thought she caught a flash of annoyance in Garth's eyes, but he passed his menu to the waitress without a word.

Once the server left, Sawyer placed his palms on the table. "Now as I was saying, we've got to find a way to—"

Bear issued his greeting bark, cutting Sawyer off before he could finish his thought. Kaylee smiled when she saw Jessica approaching their table.

"I didn't expect to find you all here," Jessica said glancing pointedly at Sawyer and Garth before briefly raising an eyebrow at Kaylee. "I heard about what happened with Gabe. I'm so sorry."

"Thanks, doll," Sawyer said. "You're ah . . ." He snapped his fingers as he fumbled for her name, and Kaylee couldn't help but wonder if they should all be wearing name tags.

"Jessica Roberts from Death by Chocolate," Jessica finished. "We're providing the cake for the wedding." She chuckled. "Five tiers, each a different flavor—vanilla, peanut butter chocolate chip, mocha, milk chocolate, and devil's food. I think it's the biggest one we've ever been asked to do. I already have six dozen molded chocolate daisies in my freezer."

"The wedding!" Sawyer slapped his hand on the table. "You're brilliant."

Jessica's eyebrows shot up. "I am?"

"I was just saying to Reese and Kaylee that I need to change course with the remainder of what we film. From here on out, we will talk about the wedding the farm is getting ready for. Josh and Savannah's wedding will erase the negativity surrounding Gabe's death. Love triumphs over tragedy at Madrona Grove." He gestured as though the words were appearing on a marquee. "Perfect."

"I'm glad I could help," Jessica said, though it was clear she wasn't sure she'd contributed something positive. "I need to go pick up my take-out order. See you all later."

As Jessica left, Sawyer's words brought to Kaylee's mind another couple who would have to triumph over the tragedy at the farm—Matt and Vanessa. She shifted uneasily. "Sawyer, are you sure that continuing to film at the farm is the best thing for the Vanguards? Their marriage seems to be strained by all the stress the show is causing."

Sawyer shrugged. "Not my problem. Matt signed a contract. We put up the money for the rehab. If they have problems, they'll need to work through them. We can't go around letting people out of contracts when they can't handle the pressure." He referenced Reese with a wave of his hand. "Too many people like the handyman here would be out a lot of money."

"I appreciate your consideration." Reese reached under the table and placed a hand on Kaylee's. "But Kaylee is right. The Vanguards' marital problems ought to be worked out before you start shoving cameras in their faces again."

"Speaking of problems," Garth said, leaning toward Reese, "Gabe mentioned that you and he had some issues in the past. Care to share what those were?"

Reese sat back in his chair. "It was a long time ago. Bygones, just like he said. I wish he hadn't brought it up."

"I imagine he did it for a reason," Sawyer said. "He did love to rile people up on camera. Half the time he didn't care one way or the other. He just knew how to lead a conversation in a certain direction to get the biggest punch. He could make something out of nothing until people were all worked up and didn't even realize they had no reason to be."

"Brilliant, really," Garth chimed in.

"I sure am going to miss that guy." Sawyer sighed. "He was one of the best in the business."

"He rarely took my cues, but I will say he knew what to do in front of a camera." Garth fiddled with his fork for a moment, then his eyes lit up. "So Reese, about your past with Gabe—was it something to do with a girl? Care to elaborate? Maybe we could use it for the show."

Reese's face darkened. "Like I said, it's ancient history."

"Oh, it definitely had something to do with a girl," Sawyer said, exchanging smirks with Garth.

Kaylee cleared her throat. "Maybe instead of trying to drum up drama where there isn't any, you should focus on undoing some of the damage you've already done." Though she knew she was on thin ice here, she couldn't help but want to fix things for Matt and Vanessa. "Why don't you hire a marriage counselor for the Vanguards or something? Instead of driving them apart, you could try to bring them closer together."

Sawyer rubbed his chin and gave Kaylee an appraising look. "You might be onto something."

"I'm glad you feel that way," Kaylee said, surprised that it hadn't taken more convincing.

Garth sat forward. "In fact, why don't *you* fix it?"

Kaylee straightened in her chair with a jolt. "Me?"

"Sure," Sawyer said. "You're pals with Vanessa, aren't you? We can schedule you for camera time with her tomorrow to take her around the garden. It'd be easy to slip some girl talk into the conversation. What do you say?"

Kaylee shook her head. "I don't feel comfortable fabricating a scene like that with her."

"Huh." Sawyer's face took on a smug cast. "You know, Garth, I was looking at our budget, and I think maybe there are a few areas where we could trim expenses."

"Oh yeah?" Garth replied. "Like where?"

"The wedding for one. Flowers sure are expensive." Sawyer stared at Kaylee, then flicked his gaze toward the restaurant door that Jessica had disappeared through a few minutes earlier. "Cakes too, come to think of it. We can definitely pick them up cheaper at a local grocery store or something."

"Are you threatening Kaylee and Jessica?" Reese demanded, his tone echoing the incredulity that washed over Kaylee.

"Not at all," Sawyer said. "I just think you ought to keep in mind the fact that we're all working for the same goal—a successful, on-time opening of Madrona Grove." He smiled, flashing artificially whitened teeth, then glanced around. "Now, where is our waitress? I think Garth and I will take our meal to go. We've got a lot of work to do."

6

With her mind pulled in a million different directions, Kaylee barely slept that night. While Bear snoozed beside her, his little legs occasionally twitching as he chased butterflies in his dreams, her thoughts pinballed from one problem to the next.

At the forefront of her concerns was Gabe's death, which the sheriff's department had been tight-lipped about. It wasn't unusual for the island's law enforcement to be discreet about a case, especially one involving a minor celebrity, but Eddie Maddox had told Kaylee that he'd be in touch with her regarding the testing of Georgine's pouch. However, more than a day after Gabe's passing, she hadn't heard a word from the sheriff.

Had they determined that Gabe had died of natural causes? Perhaps they didn't need Kaylee to examine the pouch because it wasn't evidence of anything but Georgine being in the wrong place at the wrong time. Had Gabe been sick before coming to the island? Suzy the makeup artist had complained about how hard she'd had to work to make his face camera ready, after all. Could she have been helping him camouflage the preliminary signs of illness?

Cover-ups and misdirection seemed to be the name of the game on the set of *Restaurant Restarts*. Garth, Sawyer, and Nino appeared to be comfortable fabricating the story they wanted. And now that Gabe, their resident pot stirrer, was dead, they were scrambling to find a new way to whip up excitement on set—even exploiting the ancient history of their dead host and his college buddy.

Kaylee and Reese had left O'Brien's feeling confused about

why the showrunners had wanted to dine with them. The more Kaylee thought about it, however, the more she was convinced that they had been trying to find something to exploit—namely Reese and Gabe's feud, even if it was essentially nonexistent.

And when they hadn't gotten anything out of Reese that could be used to stir up trouble on the show, they'd resorted to blackmail.

She groaned as she dragged herself out of bed at dawn to make coffee. Not sure what else to do, she had consented to being filmed talking to Vanessa about the garden. Sawyer had accepted her agreement with a wink, as if assuming she was also agreeing to grill Vanessa about the problems in her marriage. *Little chance of that happening.* Kaylee frowned as she scooped coffee into the filter and pushed the brew button. Her frown transformed into a smile when she heard the tapping of Bear's claws on the hardwood floor as he trotted into the kitchen for breakfast. She'd be leaving him at the shop with Mary for the morning, but she was glad she'd get to spend some quality time with him before dropping him off.

"Good morning, sir," she greeted. "What would you like for breakfast—kibble or kibble?"

With a happy bark, the little dog indicated that either would be just fine with him.

If only Garth were as easy to please as Bear.

"Cut!" the director shouted for what felt like the umpteenth time.

It was late morning, and Kaylee and Vanessa had been "talking casually" for more than an hour already—but apparently Kaylee wasn't very talented at holding friendly conversations on film.

"Kaylee, you're doing great, but don't worry about looking

at the camera." Garth stood behind a playback monitor, his tall frame hunched as he squinted at the footage. "Nino is an expert at setting up scenes and finding the perfect angles to make everything feel realistic and authentic."

Sawyer gave his signature smug smile. "Why don't I coach you a little bit? We'll edit out my voice later. For starters, take her through the garden plan you've got on the clipboard. After that, maybe Vanessa could ask you a few questions about caring for the plants."

Kaylee studied the clipboard in her hand for a moment, then took a deep breath and faced Vanessa, smiling at how radiant her friend appeared. Suzy had done makeup for both women, and although they still looked like themselves, their features were slightly exaggerated by Suzy's deft artistry.

After another deep breath, she nodded to Garth that she was ready. She knew what she wanted to say. She just needed to relax and be herself. But who'd have thought that being herself would be so hard?

"It feels like the whole world is watching," she muttered as Garth called for the camera to roll.

"Don't remind me," Vanessa replied under her breath. "It's what I've been saying since the beginning."

With a smile, Kaylee launched into her prepared remarks, thankfully not making any verbal missteps this time. "With an inventive menu like yours that relies heavily on farm-fresh produce, you're going to need quite a variety of seasonal fruits and vegetables to choose from."

Kaylee couldn't be sure at what point she forgot about the cameras that surrounded her and Vanessa. She went into professor mode, though this time it was with a more casual vibe. She delighted in discussing the garden with Vanessa, guiding her past the different tomatoes, leafy greens, squash, and herbs, and telling her why the vegetables had been planted where they were. "These have all been grouped with companion plants they'll thrive alongside," she explained. "It's kind of like a garden buddy system."

Sawyer cleared his throat, bringing Kaylee back to reality. "Kaylee, didn't you have something else regarding companionship you'd like to talk to Vanessa about?"

Kaylee faltered, losing her train of thought. She was still fumbling for words when she was saved, for lack of a better word, by the sound of gravel crunching under tires as a sheriff's cruiser drove down the farm's dirt lane.

While the crew watched, the car rolled to a stop by the fence. Sheriff Maddox climbed out of the driver's side, joined a moment later by Nick. Both men wore somber expressions along with their crisp uniforms.

"Can I help you, Sheriff?" Sawyer asked, an edge of petulance in his voice. "We're in the middle of shooting here."

"I can see that." Eddie strode over to the garden gate. "But if you wouldn't mind taking a short break so I can speak with Kaylee about official police business, I would appreciate it."

Sawyer's eyes narrowed, but he gave a sharp nod. "Vanessa, let's shoot some B-roll of you watering the garden."

Kaylee joined the lawmen at the gate. "What is it, Sheriff?"

Eddie indicated for her to follow him, and he led her several yards away from the garden while Nick remained at the fence. "Gabe Forester did not die of natural causes. He was poisoned."

"By accident?" she asked hopefully.

The grave expression in Eddie's eyes indicated otherwise, but he said, "I hope so. While he's waiting for test results, Giles asked for your help identifying some plants around the farm that Gabe could have come in contact with. Something that would have introduced poison into his body."

Kaylee glanced around, her gaze falling on the orchard. "I could take a walk around the property to see if I can find anything that would have poisoned Gabe, but it's only May. The plant life is barely sprouting."

Eddie nodded. "Do what you can. In the meantime, I have some questions for the crew." They returned to the garden, and the sheriff raised his voice. "Excuse me, gentlemen. I would like to talk with the crew about Gabe Forester."

"Cut!" Garth yelled angrily, his face reddened in an instant. "Can't you see we're in the middle of filming?"

Sheriff Maddox raised an eyebrow at the director. "Well, Mr. Sloan, I am in the middle of investigating a suspicious death that occurred on your set. Call me old-fashioned, but I believe that takes precedence over a television show." He inclined his head toward the camera. "And I'll be needing to see what you recorded the day Mr. Forester died."

Garth grew flustered. "I can't just turn over my footage."

"You'll get it back," Eddie said. "You have nothing to worry about. I just need to make sure there's nothing the cameras caught that we humans might have missed."

Garth glanced at Nino and shook his head. "We don't have anything to hide. Right, Nino?"

Nino pressed his lips tight and tried to stand taller, but he didn't come close to matching the sheriff's impressive height. "Nothing to hide here, but that footage needs to be protected. If anything is lost, it could mess up the show. We can't always recreate scenes. It's best to get it all on film right from the beginning. If I didn't catch it, then it never happened."

"Then I should be able to find what killed Gabe," the sheriff said smoothly. "Because the man is dead, and that *did* happen."

Nino's shoulders slumped as the fight went out of him. "We can go into the production trailer to view the footage."

While Garth and Nino accompanied the sheriff to the production trailer, Nick remained behind with Kaylee. "So do you think there's some poisonous plant around here that Forester might have eaten?" he asked her.

"It's possible," Kaylee said. "The symptoms he displayed remind me of zygacine poisoning. It's a steroidal alkaloid found in several species of plant known as death camas. Those have killed people who mistook them for edible plants like wild onion, as well as sheep and cattle who have picked up death camas while grazing. Gabe would have had no reason to be foraging for edible plants, so I don't know how he would have come into contact with it."

"You were on set that day, right? Did you see him eat anything?"

Kaylee flicked a glance at Vanessa, who had been lingering in the garden since the sheriff had left. The chef's face was flushed, and her fists were clenched. Clearly she'd overheard Nick's questions.

"Gabe ate several of my dishes, as I'm sure you know," Vanessa said as she stomped through the garden toward the deputy. "And he didn't enjoy a single one, including my Veggie Vigor juice."

"Juice?" Nick repeated. "You could blend just about anything into that, couldn't you? Even something poisonous, like this death camas stuff?"

Vanessa shook her head. "Don't be ridiculous."

"Maybe you didn't mean to put it in," he suggested. "Maybe it was mixed up with the other vegetables."

"Holly brought the vegetables from her greenhouse," Kaylee said. "I've been there a hundred times, and she doesn't have anything resembling death camas growing in there. Besides, she's careful and a professional. She would be able to identify death camas and keep it out of her produce."

Nick rubbed his goatee. "Ms. Sampson has been accused of poisoning before."

"That's not fair, Nick," Kaylee argued. "You know full well she did no such thing."

"What?" Tears welled up in Vanessa's eyes. "I trusted Holly's vegetables until mine were grown." She swiped at her cheek, leaving a streak of mud across it. "I've been too trusting of everyone. Even my own husband went behind my back." She stomped her foot. "And I'm the one who ends up paying the price. Matt trusted this show, but I'm the one who suffered Gabe's insults. Now Gabe's dead, and the woman I trusted for food may have set me up to take the fall? I don't deserve any of this."

Vanessa spun on her heel and headed for the cow pasture. Kaylee had noticed that she went there a lot for solace. *Or is it for something else?*

As Kaylee scanned the fields, an idea began to form. In addition to death camas, there were plenty of other poisonous plants associated with cows, and one in particular stuck in her mind.

"She seems upset," Nick said, drawing Kaylee's attention back to him.

Kaylee rolled her eyes. "And they wonder why you're still single. You do realize you're the one who upset her, right?"

"Who, me?" Nick shrugged. "I'm just doing my job."

"Stirring the pot to see what floats to the top? Insinuating that Holly of all people could have had a hand in Gabe's death? I don't remember you using that kind of underhanded tactic before."

"That seems to be what these Hollywood types respond to, unfortunately."

"Vanessa isn't a Hollywood type."

"Maybe it was an accident."

"That's entirely possible."

Kaylee walked to the edge of the garden. Nick followed,

but remained quiet, waiting for her to elaborate on how Gabe's poisoning could have been accidental. Kaylee wasn't sure if she was on to something or way off, but she felt that the idea was worth voicing.

"There's a plant called white snakeroot that shoots up in the spring," she said. "It poisons rangelands for cattle. Most farmers know to clear their pastures of the plant, which is a member of the aster family. If the cattle eat it, they will get sick, but more importantly, their milk becomes toxic. Deadly even. And no pasteurization will deactivate the poison."

"If the Vanguards are new to raising cows, they might not know about keeping the pastures clear," Nick said.

Kaylee nodded. "I'll go talk to Vanessa and check the land."

"Want me to come?" Nick offered.

"I'm not sure she'll open up much if you're around." Kaylee offered a smile. "No offense. It might be best if I talk to her alone."

Nick nodded. "Good luck."

"Thanks," Kaylee said, though she wasn't sure if good fortune would be finding the snakeroot or not.

She made her way through the tall grass that separated the garden from the cow pasture. Ahead, Vanessa leaned forward on the fence with her back to Kaylee. Kaylee approached carefully but not silently. She didn't want to sneak up on the already tense woman.

"Do you have a few minutes to chat?" Kaylee asked when she joined the other woman at the railing.

Vanessa didn't reply at first, but eventually she nodded.

"Deputy Durham didn't mean to upset you," Kaylee said. "He's just trying to figure out what caused Gabe's death. And so am I."

Vanessa frowned. "You?"

"From time to time, the sheriff asks me to help with a case that involves plants."

"Like Holly's poisonous vegetables?" The chef's tart tone made it obvious that she hadn't forgotten what Nick had said.

"Sort of," Kaylee said carefully. She scanned the land in front of her. "Abraham Lincoln's mother died from something called milk sickness. Have you ever heard of it?"

"It doesn't sound familiar."

"Lots of folks actually died from it before people began to realize the sickness was coming from the cows, and that the victims were being poisoned through their milk."

"My cows are fine," Vanessa shot back. "Look at them. They are healthy and strong."

"They do seem happy," Kaylee agreed, watching the cluster of mild-mannered cattle grazing. "Sometimes it's the older and younger cattle that are affected. Their limbs will tremble if they've eaten snakeroot."

"Snakeroot?"

"That's right. White snakeroot, to be specific. It's native to the eastern half of the country, but it's also an invasive species that can adapt to multiple environments, so it could have been introduced here. If the cows eat it, it can taint their milk with a toxin called tremetol, which gets people sick." Kaylee took a breath. "It could kill them."

"And you think Gabe drank the cows' milk and died from snakeroot poisoning?"

"I remember him eating some mozzarella on a salad. You made that, right?"

Vanessa's face flushed with horror. "But we only use milk we've pasteurized for the cheese-making process."

"It wouldn't matter. Pasteurization doesn't affect the toxin." Kaylee placed a gentle hand on her friend's shoulder. "Don't panic yet. We don't even know if there is snakeroot in these fields. I'd like to check, if you don't mind."

Vanessa shrugged and waved her hand forward. "Have at it. Tell me what to watch for, and I'll help."

"Actually, that's a good idea." Kaylee removed her phone from her pants pocket. She pulled up a search engine and requested an image of the plant. "They have a cluster of white flowers that can kind of resemble those of onion flowers, but we won't see those yet, as they don't bloom until late summer or early autumn." She handed the phone to Vanessa. "This is in full bloom, but if you scroll, you'll see it in its shoots stage as well. As a farmer, you're going to want to know what to look for because it is a dangerous plant for your cows to eat. You're going to need to be sure you walk your land starting in the spring and pull up any snakeroot you see."

Vanessa returned the phone, then the two women made their way through the gate and into the field. Cows grazed all around them, ignoring their presence for the most part. A few lifted their heavy heads to peer at them with droopy eyes, but soon went back to eating.

"Why do they call it snakeroot?" Vanessa asked.

"A poultice made from its roots was once used to draw out snake venom," Kaylee answered as she crouched down to start her inspection. "It was an old practice handed down from indigenous people, but it's not used much these days. Scientists are iffy on whether it actually worked."

"Well, I would think not, especially if it kills through milk." Vanessa mirrored Kaylee's actions. "How scary."

Kaylee ran her hand across the wispy grass, searching for evidence of the plant. "Believe it or not, lots of different plants are called snakeroot, and many have been used for a variety of medicinal purposes. There's even a species that's supposed to help with fertility."

"Fertility?" Vanessa froze with her hand over the grass. "How does it help with that?"

"That's still being investigated, but it's thought to affect the release of hormones that make it easier to get pregnant."

"Huh." Vanessa glanced back toward the barn and trailers. "If you don't mind, I forgot something was cooking in my trailer. I need to check on it."

Kaylee frowned in confusion. Vanessa hadn't mentioned anything about cooking while they were in the garden. "That's fine. I'll keep searching. But so far, I don't see any sign of the plant."

"Good. That's good," Vanessa said absently as she stood and rushed back to the gate.

Sheriff Maddox was entering as Vanessa ran past him. He nodded to her, then watched her retreat before approaching Kaylee.

"I swapped with Nick. He can watch that footage. It's painful, the way they captured every moment." Eddie shook his head. "But that increases our chances of seeing what Forester ate that killed him."

"I hope it helps narrow down where he got the plant. I don't see any evidence of snakeroot here." At a questioning glance from Eddie, she repeated to him what she'd told Nick about the plant.

"The name sounds sneaky and underhanded, like a snake in the grass," he said. "And I'm thinking that's what happened to Gabe."

"You mean murder?" Kaylee felt a chill despite the warm morning sun shining on her shoulders. "You really think he was killed? But who would have done something like that?"

Eddie gave Kaylee a wry smile. "If I put any credence in Georgine Snowbird's claims, there are a whole host of angry spirits who would be up for the task."

With another shiver, Kaylee wondered if the herbalist had given Gabe snakeroot. Had she carried some in her pouch? "If you'd still like me to examine her pouch, I can," Kaylee told the sheriff.

"That'd be helpful," he said. "But it might be a better use of your time to come with me tomorrow to Georgine's house. You can tell me if she's got anything dangerous in her collection of herbs."

"Sure," Kaylee said, hoping her tone didn't reveal her reluctance. She'd been eager to see Georgine's collection of herbs when she'd first met her—but that was before the sheriff had insinuated that the Lummi herbalist could be using her botanical knowledge not to heal . . . but to kill.

7

Although Georgine Snowbird's property was within walking distance of Madrona Grove, its surroundings proved how quickly Orcas Island's terrain could change. The simple log home sat high up on a hill along the island's northwestern coast, giving Georgine a majestic panorama featuring ocean in one direction and forest in another.

Between forest and ocean, tall grasses mixed with the spring mounds of lavender that would become a pretty purple come late June and July. It would sway along the side of the hills down to the rocky shoreline like the rolling waves themselves.

"I see where she harvests her lavender," Kaylee said to the sheriff as he put his cruiser in park in front of the house. He had picked her up at The Flower Patch, where she'd left Bear in Mary's care. "She has it in abundance." She searched beyond the tidy, one-story home for other plants. "With such a variety of terrain, she could be growing every kind of plant, from full sun to total shade."

Eddie shut the car off and opened his door. "We're only interested in the poisonous ones."

They made their way up to the front door. The sheriff knocked and rang the doorbell, but after receiving no response, he said, "Maybe she's around back."

They found Georgine hanging sheets on a clothesline in the yard. The breeze coming off the water whipped the cotton, snapping it and making it billow around her. She wore the same striped coat she'd had on at the farm the other day. With her back to Kaylee and the sheriff, she didn't realize they were there until she reached for another clothespin from the basket behind her.

Georgine paused when she spotted them, then returned to her work. She unhurriedly clipped the last clothespin on the line and scooped up the empty basket under one arm. She made her way toward them at a slow pace and stopped a few feet away.

"Sheriff." Georgine's voice was serene, though her eyes were wary. "How can I help you?" She tucked a long, wispy strand of black hair behind her ear as her gaze flitted back and forth between Eddie and Kaylee.

"I have a few questions pertaining to your plants," Maddox said. "Do you have some time?"

Georgine nodded, but confusion flickered on her face. "What do you want to know about my plants?"

"I'll defer to my forensic botanist on that, actually." Eddie gestured for Kaylee to take the lead.

"I thought you were a florist," Georgine said, her eyes narrowing.

"I am. But there's more to plants than putting them in vases, as I'm sure you know." Kaylee glanced around the yard, spotting several gardens in various stages of development and growth. "We were wondering if you had any snakeroot in your possession."

Georgine's gaze slid to her right. Kaylee followed and saw a large garden of perennials, including lily of the valley and tiger lilies, beginning to grow.

"They're just starting to come up," Georgine said as she pointed to a cluster of tiny sticklike shoots protruding from the earth. "They will have cream-colored flowers and curve like long, thin snakes when they are in full bloom."

"That's *Zigadenus densus*," Kaylee blurted, then explained, "It's a death camas known as black snakeroot, a member of the lily family. And it's not native to the Pacific Northwest."

"I grow many plants that aren't native, including another form of snakeroot called black cohosh," Georgine said. "The world is wide and full of wonders."

Maddox scrutinized the shoots for a moment. "Do you have any that are further along than this?"

Georgine shook her head. "You can't rush nature."

"What about white snakeroot?" Kaylee asked.

The herbalist looked into the trees that her land abutted. "Come fall, there will be white snakeroot growing in the forest. You won't see any sign of it now, but its roots are there, under the earth."

"Did you give Gabe Forester any plants to eat before he died?" the sheriff asked.

Georgine frowned. "I told you everything at the farm."

"Just tell me again," Eddie said.

Georgine pursed her lips, appearing as though she didn't want to answer. Finally, she did. "None at all."

He rubbed his jaw. "Why were you with him in the kitchen trailer?"

"I've told you all of this already. I brought Mr. Forester a collection that would ward off the harmful spirits, but he spurned it. Why are you making me repeat myself?" Georgine began walking toward her home at a brisker pace than Kaylee had seen her use before.

Sheriff Maddox kept up with the herbalist, and Kaylee followed. "Because a man is dead," Eddie said, "and it's my job to figure out why."

Georgine glanced over her shoulder. "Come with me, then. I'll show you my collection of dried plants. It's in my root cellar."

Georgine guided them to a door at the back of her house. Once opened, a set of rickety stairs led down to an orderly assemblage of cabinets and small sets of drawers. Crates and boxes lined the walls. Thick, wooden beams along the low ceiling displayed bundled herbs in various stages of drying.

A consortium of smells, some of them rather foul, assaulted Kaylee's senses. She was used to the sweet perfumes at The Flower Patch, not this mix of odors from more utilitarian plants. Most of the plants were in their dying state, their decaying aroma unlike their living scent.

Clearly aware of Kaylee's discomfort, Georgine said, "You get used to it."

"I can't place the smell," Kaylee admitted.

"I can," Sheriff Maddox said. "Are you sure there's not a dead body in here?"

Georgine appeared amused. "Positive. It's skunk cabbage." She pointed to a cluster of waxy yellow flowers with thick, spiky spadix resting on a table.

"*Lysichiton americanus*?" Kaylee was surprised. "You really do have everything in here."

"It can be made into a poultice for treating wounds," Georgine explained, "though the odor can be a bit harsh."

The sheriff crinkled his nose. "You can say that again."

The herbalist shrugged. "It will be better down here after I process it."

"I'll take your word for it. I hope not to bother you again," Sheriff Maddox said. "Assuming you didn't give Gabe any snakeroot."

"There was no snakeroot in the bag I tried to give him, but I have plenty of it down here." Georgine tapped a set of drawers. "I have both white and black that I collected last year and dried for future use."

Kaylee frowned, wondering what use Georgine might have for a plant as deadly as *Zigadenus densus*.

Georgine ran her fingers along a row of drawers, then stopped. She pulled one wooden drawer all the way out and set it down onto a worn pine worktable. She moved aside a large mortar and pestle, placing it under the table on a shelf of others just like it.

Kaylee and the sheriff peered into the long box, which held dried brown pellets that resembled tiny wood chips.

"Would you let us take a sample?" Eddie asked. "I'd also like to take whatever you were trying to give Mr. Forester."

Georgine eyed them both warily. "I get the feeling you're trying to establish my guilt."

"Or innocence," Maddox countered. "The coroner believes the deceased was poisoned, though he hasn't identified the toxin yet."

Georgine's face stilled and hardened. "Whatever it was, I didn't give it to him. I think I want a lawyer." She picked up the box and inserted it back into its slot, then rounded on Kaylee and the sheriff. "And you'll need a warrant to confiscate any of my plants—dried or fresh leaves, roots, or bulbs. I won't be turning over anything today. I know my rights. I've fought for many who have been used and taken advantage of. Even the dead." Georgine moved to the door to show them the way out. As Kaylee and Sheriff Maddox passed her, she said, "And if you ask me, Gabe Forester was killed by angry spirits."

Eddie paused. "I'm afraid I can't lead an investigation based on the warnings of angry spirits that only you think exist. Right now, I have to work off the assumption that Gabe Forester died from ingesting a poisonous plant—possibly one that you possess."

Georgine waved a hand at the bins and drawers. "I have poisonous plants by the dozen. I have never killed anyone with them. I know which ones to keep under lock and key. I know how much is safe. No one has ever died by using my medicinal herbs. I will let my record vouch for me in front of any judge. Now, I think it's time for you to go."

Sheriff Maddox gave a stiff nod, then took the first steps up and out, followed by Kaylee and Georgine.

Outside, Georgine closed the door behind them. "I do hope you figure out where Mr. Forester came into contact with poison," she said as she walked them around to the front of the house. "Even if I had given him some, it wouldn't have been enough to kill him." She stopped when the cruiser came into view. "If I were you, I'd look to the land. That is where the spirits will work from, maybe by making white snakeroot grow in the cows' pasture. If cows have eaten it, the poison will show up in their milk."

"I considered that already," Kaylee said. "Yesterday I searched for signs of the plant in the pasture, but I didn't find any."

"Look to the cows," the herbalist insisted. "You may not have been able to find any because they've already eaten it. If they've ingested any, it will cause tremors in their legs. The earth and its creatures hold the answers. They will tell you how this happened."

Kaylee gazed into Georgine's eyes. "Believe me when I tell you, I do not think you purposely killed Gabe."

Georgine's face remained stony. "Nor did I accidentally kill him. Keep examining the farm. Your answers will come from there." She walked to her front door and opened it, but paused and fixed her focus on the sheriff. "If you come back, make sure it's with a warrant. Otherwise, don't bother."

The door closed behind her with a gentle click.

Kaylee sighed as she walked the rest of the way to the car. "I really don't think she killed anyone."

Eddie opened the passenger door for Kaylee to climb in. Before he shut it, he glanced at the house. "She didn't want to offer a sample either. If she's innocent, why not help? Especially when she knows so much."

"It's because she's smart that she didn't offer to help," Kaylee said. "She knows something could be used against her. Another reason I have doubts about her guilt. I believe her when she says she knows her plants and their purposes and dosages. She takes her role as herbalist for her people very seriously. She would be letting many people down if she killed someone. Her own tribe wouldn't be able to trust her anymore."

Eddie hummed a noncommittal response.

"With your blessing," Kaylee continued, "I'm going to keep searching the land, like she said. If I can find snakeroot shoots at the farm, that'll help take the focus off Georgine."

"Maybe." Sheriff Maddox shut Kaylee's door and walked around the front of the car. After he climbed in and shut his own door, he started the engine. But before he put the car in gear, he glanced over at the log home. "But I can't reject any possibilities just yet."

Just before the sheriff dropped Kaylee off at The Flower Patch, he asked her if she'd have time the next day to test the interior of Georgine's leather pouch for evidence of any poisonous plants that could have caused Gabe's death. Hopeful that examining the pouch would help exonerate the herbalist, Kaylee agreed readily, promising to meet a deputy at Akin Funeral Chapel first thing in the morning. She had a microscope at the flower shop, but in this case it made more sense for her to use the coroner's equipment, since the rest of the evidence was already in his lab at the chapel.

With the time set, Kaylee said goodbye and climbed out of the cruiser. As she entered the front door of the shop, she nearly tripped over someone crouched down beside the sales display of

DeeDee's handmade goat milk soap. "Whoa," she said, stopping just before she collided with the person.

"Sorry, I'm in the way," Matt Vanguard said, straightening up. He'd been petting Bear, and the dog released a joyful bark and scurried over to Kaylee for some affection from her.

"If you're giving Bear attention, you're not in the way," she said lightly as she greeted a wiggling Bear with an ear rub.

Matt grinned at Bear. "It'd be awesome to have a working dog on the farm." The smile fell off his face. "Better discuss it with Vanessa first, though."

"It would be a big decision to make without her input," Kaylee said carefully, knowing that Matt's impulsive decisions were already causing friction for the couple.

He laughed mirthlessly. "No kidding. I'm on thin ice with her." He glanced around. "In fact, that's why I'm here. I know it's a cliché, but I'm hoping a bouquet of flowers will get me out of the doghouse."

"Bouquets that get husbands out of the doghouse are one of our specialties."

"Can I get out of the doghouse for twenty bucks? It's about all I can afford to spend right now."

"I imagine so." Kaylee led him to the cooler. "Do you see anything in here she'd like? If not, Mary or I can make something for you."

Matt examined the case for a few moments, then pointed to an elaborate arrangement of pink and white roses. "Those look just like her wedding bouquet." He sighed. "We thought we had it all figured out back then. We'd work in L.A. for a few years, save up some money, then buy a farm where we could open our restaurant."

"That's exactly what you're doing," Kaylee said. "You ought to be proud of yourselves."

"What's there to be proud of? We bought the farm sight unseen, without an inspection, and we ended up spending our entire nest egg on a new septic system. I had to find a way to keep our dream alive, which is why I signed the contract with *Restaurant Restarts*. Turns out, I was selling my soul. I wouldn't mind if it was going well and Vanessa was happy. But she's miserable, and it's my fault."

Kaylee's heart went out to Matt. He may have made a misstep, but it was all in the name of love. "You were just trying to keep your dream alive. Nobody can fault you for that."

Matt snorted derisively. "Vanessa certainly does. None of our dreams are coming true. It's more like a nightmare." He closed his eyes momentarily, pain washing over his face. "She's so distraught, Kaylee. She's upset about Gabe's death, and she's even more worried that her food had something to do with it. And now she's got it in her mind that our cows might have ingested some weed that poisoned their milk." He heaved a sigh. "I don't know how to make this right."

Kaylee reached into the cooler for the vase of roses. As she pulled it out, she remembered what Georgine had said about cows that ingested snakeroot. "Are any of your cows suffering from tremors?"

Confused, Matt shook his head. "No. Why?"

"The plant Vanessa is worried about is called snakeroot. It can cause tremors in cows who eat it and poison their milk." Kaylee closed the cooler door. "Have you milked your cows today?"

"Ugh, thanks for reminding me." The young farmer's shoulders slumped. "Another disaster. I milked them all right—all by myself because my assistant quit. He said he didn't want to work on a cursed farm that's losing money by the minute."

Kaylee grimaced in sympathy. "I'm so sorry."

"That's not all. Reese ran into trouble with the electric in the barn, so I don't have a refrigerator to store it in. I had to dump it all." Matt groaned. "Maybe Madrona Grove really is cursed. Sure would explain a lot."

"I don't believe in curses," Kaylee said, putting the vase into Matt's hands. "You've had a run of bad luck, but you're trying your hardest."

Matt read the tag on the arrangement and his eyes widened. "That's out of my price range." He tried to hand it back to Kaylee, but she shook her head.

"You said twenty dollars, right? I think that's fair. It's what Mary and I call the special. You and Vanessa could use some grace."

"Thanks, Kaylee." Matt beamed at her, the first time he'd seemed genuinely happy in a long time. "I won't forget the favor. If I can ever return it, let me know."

"Actually, there is something I need to ask your permission to do." At Matt's questioning expression, she explained, "I'd like to test your cows' milk. If I find evidence of snakeroot in it, that could mean that it poisoned Gabe."

"But then it'd be an accident, right? Vanessa would never have known the milk was poisoned."

"Precisely."

Matt practically bounced on his toes in anticipation. "If you can prove that it's not Vanessa's fault, it'll be a huge weight off her shoulders. How early can you pick up a sample?"

"I'd love to be able to alleviate her worries," Kaylee said hesitantly. "But you should prepare yourself for either outcome." She realized that she could test the milk at the funeral chapel at the same time she was testing Georgine's pouch. "Actually, it would probably be better if I took my own sample, so I can vouch that it came straight from the source and wasn't doctored in any way. I trust you, but it might need to hold up in court. Is that all right?"

After a brief hesitation, Matt nodded. "I'm usually out there at four if you want to join me."

"In the morning?" Kaylee only knew one other person who got up that early. In fact . . . "I'll be there. And I'll bring a friend."

8

"I can't believe you convinced me to do this," Jessica grumbled as she climbed into Kaylee's SUV at quarter to four the next morning. She put on her seat belt, then settled an enthusiastic Bear onto her lap. "It's the middle of the night."

"Come on, you're a baker," Kaylee said as she reversed out of the driveway. "You're always up early. And that's for you." She pointed to a travel mug she'd filled with coffee. It wouldn't be as good as the coffee Jessica made at Death by Chocolate, but hopefully it would take the edge off.

"Not *this* early," Jessica muttered, taking a sip from the mug. "Could you remind me again why you so generously thought I'd enjoy coming with you?"

"Would you be offended if I told you I invited you in case I need a diversion?"

Jessica arched a suspicious eyebrow. "I thought Matt knew you were coming."

"He's not the one I need a diversion from. I don't want anyone else to know that I'm taking the milk sample, especially Sawyer or Garth. The last thing the Vanguards need is the showrunners fabricating another scandal where there isn't one." Kaylee bit her lip. "Or at least I hope there isn't one."

"And you're hoping this sample will prove that Gabe contracted something called milk sickness?" Jessica asked.

Kaylee nodded. "It's the simplest explanation, and no one would be held responsible. If it's not that, then there's something sinister going on. It could mean someone killed him on purpose."

"Unless Vanessa poisoned the cows intentionally," Jessica

said, shooting Kaylee a worried look. Then she shook her head. "Nah. Even I know how unlikely that is. She'd never be that cruel. Besides, what if someone else drank the milk or whatever they made from it? I don't think she would have risked that."

Kaylee smiled. Jessica had a healthy appreciation for conspiracy theories, but she also had a grip on reality. "If the cows are poisoned, it wouldn't be on purpose. Or at least, that's what I hope. I read up on milk sickness last night. Death could happen in the young calves and the older cows, but the Vanguards' herd is pretty strong. Still, they can experience side effects from the poison. I'm going to keep an eye out for tremors in the cows' legs."

"I have to say this is one of the weirdest things you've ever had me do," Jessica said as Kaylee turned onto the gravel drive leading to the farm. "And yet, I'm strangely excited."

The SUV's tires crunched as they pulled up to the barn and parked beside it. Not a single light burned in the barn, in the farmhouse, or in any of the trailers. The last part wasn't surprising since the crew were all lodging in rentals down the road, but if Matt was awake, surely there'd be some sign of him. Kaylee checked the car's digital clock, which read four on the dot. Had she misheard him?

"Wow!" Jessica exclaimed, pointing to a new patio jutting off the side of the barn. Orange caution cones outlined the patio, and a few cones were also set up in front of the barn's main doors. "Did that go in since Sunday?"

"Reese said the concrete was just poured yesterday." Kaylee reached over and clipped a leash on Bear. "They stamped it to make it look like bricks."

Jessica cooed appreciatively as she and Kaylee climbed out of the car. "It'll be hard to decide whether to dine in the barn or out in nature. I guess that just means Luke and I will have to be regulars so we get to try both."

I just hope the restaurant gets to open so you have that opportunity. Kaylee didn't voice her concerns, though. She needed to stay positive if she was going to help clear the way for Madrona Grove to open on time—for the sake of the Vanguards and the couple planning to be married there soon. Kaylee's step faltered. *But if the milk is poisoned, what happens then?*

"Hey, are you sure we should be here?" Jessica asked, glancing around warily. "It doesn't seem like anybody is doing any milking right now."

"Matt knows we're coming. Maybe he just overslept."

Jessica rubbed her arms against the slight chill in the early morning air. "Should we wait here or go over to the pasture and wait for him there?"

Kaylee glanced toward the cow enclosure. "Let's head over. It will give us time to observe the cows without anyone noticing."

With Bear leading the way, Kaylee and Jessica walked to the pasture, where the small herd huddled together quietly on the near side of the enclosure. The moon was full and still high, casting the docile animals in a white glow. The friends stood shoulder to shoulder at the fence and watched the cattle for a few minutes.

"I don't see any sign of tremors in their legs," Kaylee finally said softly, not wanting to disturb the peaceful scene.

"That's good." Jessica frowned. "Or is that bad? We don't want the cows suffering, but we do want milk sickness to be the cause of Gabe's death, because that way it was likely an accident, and at least we know what happened. Right?"

"When you put it that way . . ." Kaylee exhaled.

Apparently done sniffing the grass, Bear came and sat at her feet, his warm little body resting against her ankles.

"I should have worn a thicker coat." Jessica rubbed her arms again. "I hope Matt gets here soon, or else I'll need to figure out how to get the milk out myself. But how hard could it be? Squeeze and pull, right?"

Kaylee laughed. "I'm not sure it's that easy."

"Sure it is," Matt said as he approached.

Kaylee hadn't heard his footsteps, and her pulse quickened slightly at the surprise of finding him there. "Good morning, Matt."

"Sorry I'm a little late," he said. "Ready?"

"As we'll ever be," Jessica said brightly.

With Matt's guidance, Jessica and Kaylee helped him lead three cows to the working area of the barn, where milking stalls were set up. Following his instructions, they milked the cows into shiny metal buckets. Kaylee was hesitant at first, but she soon got the hang of it and was ready to move on to her second cow in less than fifteen minutes.

"Not bad for a beginner," Matt said when he came over to check on her. "You too, Jessica. If you're looking for part-time work, I'm hiring."

Kaylee chuckled. "I think I've got plenty of jobs to keep me busy already. Speaking of which, do you mind if I take samples from these three cows before we do the others?"

"No problem," Matt said. "Do your thing."

Kaylee retrieved a pair of surgical gloves, a marker, three vials, and three disposable plastic syringes from her tote. She labeled each vial with the name of one of the cows currently being milked—Nellie, Stardust, and Banana—then put on the gloves and pulled samples from each bucket, using a different syringe each time.

The trio repeated the process with the remaining cows, and soon Kaylee had six milk samples to test later that morning. As the sun started peeking over the horizon, they returned the last three cows—Amber, Viola, and Caramel—to the pasture.

"I can't thank you ladies enough," Matt said as he pulled the gate shut behind them.

"It was no trouble," Jessica said, suppressing a yawn while they strolled back toward the barn. "I've always wanted to learn how to milk a cow—not that I plan on making a habit of it."

Matt laughed, and Kaylee thought the farmer seemed less burdened than he had previously. "It's not just the milking, though I do appreciate that," he said. "I honestly am mostly thankful for your kindness, both to me and to Vanessa. This whole experience with *Restaurant Restarts* has taught me that not everyone is looking out for their neighbor. Plenty of people are just out for themselves."

"Not everybody, though." Kaylee breathed in the fresh morning air and marveled at the beautiful pinks and oranges spreading across the sky. "The crew will be gone soon, and you and Vanessa will settle into real life on Orcas Island. You'll be able to forget all about the bad stuff and focus on the good."

"I hope you're right," Matt said, then groaned. Nino had appeared around the side of the barn, the camera on his shoulder aimed directly at them. "But I think being part of the show is going to haunt me for a long, long time."

After dropping Jessica off at home so she could shower quickly before heading to Death by Chocolate just in time to open for the day, Kaylee returned to Wildflower Cottage to get clean herself. She had the luxury of taking a bit more time getting ready, and as she washed up with DeeDee's goat milk soap, she smiled to herself. *Now that I've mastered milking cows, maybe goats should be next.*

She received a text from Nick letting her know that he'd meet her at Akin Funeral Chapel shortly with Georgine's pouch.

Dressed in cropped pants and a boatneck tee, she grabbed the milk samples and headed out into the sunny morning with Bear. Once she had dropped him off at The Flower Patch, where she knew he'd nap until Mary arrived a little bit later, she walked the few blocks to Akin Funeral Chapel.

Just inside the A-frame building's front door, a familiar face at the visitor's check-in stand welcomed her with a smile. The solemn sound of organ music floated out from the chapel, and Kaylee cringed, thinking she'd walked in on a memorial service.

Thelma Akin clearly knew what Kaylee was thinking. "Don't worry, dear," Giles's wife and right-hand woman at the funeral home said brightly. "Giles is just auditioning a substitute organist. Poor Mr. Bender broke his right wrist."

"I'm sorry to hear that." Kaylee listened to the music for a moment. "Whoever this is sounds like they're up to the task of filling in."

Thelma nodded, her auburn hair bouncing. "It's Greg Simmons, if you can believe it."

Actually, Kaylee couldn't believe it. Greg was a teenager who lived in Eastsound, a larger village on the island, and his mother ran a competing florist shop called Simmons Kind of Wonderful. "I didn't realize he played the organ."

"People have a way of surprising us, don't they? Even teenagers." Thelma chuckled, then pointed down the carpeted hall. "Nick is already in the lab waiting for you. I don't think organ music is his cup of tea." She put her hand beside her mouth and added in a stage whisper, "Though if it happened to be Marnie Galt playing, I think he'd make an exception."

Kaylee laughed. "You might be right about that." Marnie Galt taught music at the Turtle Cove elementary school, coached sailing at the high school, and had in no uncertain terms told Nick, a shameless flirt, that she wouldn't date him unless they were exclusive. Nick was doing his level best to convince the pretty, thirtysomething blonde that he only had eyes for her.

"Giles has something he needs to discuss with you when he's done with Greg," Thelma said. "Make sure you don't leave without talking to him."

"Thanks, Thelma." Kaylee walked down the hall and stepped into Giles's lab, where Nick sat on a rolling stool, a plastic evidence bag in his hands. "Good morning, Nick. I heard you're in here hiding from the organ music."

"More like hiding from the Akin Inquisition," Nick replied with a smirk. "She was giving me the third degree about Marnie Galt."

Kaylee arched an eyebrow. "Your feelings about Marnie are Orcas Island's worst kept secret. Any progress?"

Nick shot her a boyish grin. "I've been upgraded from 'no' to 'maybe.'"

"Sounds promising."

"Actually, it is." Nick stood up and offered Kaylee the evidence bag. "The sheriff asked me to deliver this and wait for the results."

Kaylee nodded and accepted the bag. "Do you have a little extra time? If so, you can stay while I test some milk samples I got from Madrona Grove. If the cows there ingested snakeroot, it could affect their milk, and it could have poisoned Gabe."

"Does the sheriff know you're doing this?"

"I told him I was going to look for evidence of snakeroot at the farm, and this is in line with that. And I have permission from Matt Vanguard. He helped me get the samples this morning."

Amusement colored the deputy's face. "What'd you do, milk the cows yourself?"

Kaylee straightened her posture and offered a proud smile. "As a matter of fact, I did."

While Nick chuckled in amusement and returned to his stool, Kaylee took out her phone and brought up the reference images she'd saved of various kinds of snakeroot at a microscopic level. Confident that she could recognize snakeroot on sight, she put on disposable gloves and removed the leather pouch from the plastic bag. As she placed it under the microscope, she hoped that she wouldn't find any evidence of poisonous plants on the leather, then chided herself. *I'm representing law enforcement with this exam. I can't let my feelings cloud my judgment.*

As it turned out, Kaylee's concerns about her judgment being clouded were for nothing. Although microscopic evidence of lavender, chamomile, sage, and other herbs clung to the leather, the pouch showed no sign of having ever contained snakeroot.

"There's no black or white snakeroot visible," she told Nick as she wrote up a report. "Hopefully that means Georgine Snowbird moves down the suspect list."

Nick shrugged noncommittally, but he pulled out his phone and dashed off a quick text that Kaylee suspected was to Eddie Maddox.

Next, Kaylee went about prepping six milk slides, labeling each with the donor cow's name, then placed Nellie's sample under the microscope. With her eye to the viewer, Kaylee scrutinized the sample, but found no evidence of white snakeroot.

She repeated the process for the other five slides, but she saw nothing that warranted further examination or breakdown. All of the cows' milk appeared normal and healthy.

"Well that was a dead end," she said grumpily as she cleaned up the work area and disposed of the slides. "The milk didn't poison Gabe."

"No, it didn't."

At the sound of Giles's voice, Kaylee and Nick spun to face the lab doorway, where the funeral director stood with a lab report.

"Do you still suspect foul play?" Giles's keen hazel eyes were shining, and he was more animated than his usual reserved self. "If so, I think I've got your murder weapon right here."

9

"Murder weapon?" Nick repeated, jumping up from his stool. "What do you mean?"

Giles entered the room and closed the door behind him. "First of all, Kaylee, can you please confirm how black snakeroot starts out? Is it seeds or bulbs?"

"Bulbs," she answered. "Why?"

"I mislabeled something in Mr. Forester's stomach," the coroner said. "During the autopsy, I categorized the contents, and nothing seemed out of the ordinary. Of course I still had the contents tested, especially when I couldn't identify the poison that killed him." Giles adjusted his glasses. "It turns out I was wrong."

Kaylee frowned. "Wrong that Gabe was poisoned?"

"No, I was wrong about what was in his stomach." Giles waved the paper in his hand. "I thought he had eaten an onion. I didn't even think twice, just labeled it a pearl onion and moved on. But it turns out that was what killed him."

"Onions aren't poisonous," Nick said. "Unless you know something I don't." He glanced between Kaylee and Giles, then laughed. "Which I'm sure you two do."

Giles smiled wanly. "He didn't eat an onion."

"Yes he did." Kaylee remembered the moment Gabe had tried Vanessa's Veggie Vigor juice. "I watched him bite it off a long toothpick garnishing the glass of vegetable juice. He complained it tasted horrible."

"That wasn't an onion," Giles said again. "The poison came back identified as zygacine, the alkaloid produced by death camas, which means what I thought was an onion was actually—"

"A bulb!" Kaylee exclaimed, putting two and two together. "Gabe ate a black snakeroot bulb." Horror immediately overtook her. "Someone must have put it on that skewer."

Kaylee's mind immediately bounced from one potential culprit to the next. Georgine certainly had access to bulbs, and she'd been lurking around the farm that day, even before following Gabe into the kitchen trailer before he died. But Kaylee still wasn't convinced that Georgine had much of a motive. *Unless she was so desperate to get everyone off the so-called cursed land that she orchestrated a death.*

Shaking her head, Kaylee moved on to another suspicious person she didn't want to be guilty — Vanessa. The chef certainly had ill feelings toward Gabe, who had publicly derided her food, and she wasn't shy about sharing her contempt for the fact that she'd been unwittingly swept up into the filming of a reality show. Besides, the fact of the matter was that she'd been the one to make the juice — had she been the one to garnish and serve it, though?

The TV crew was large, and any one of the various assistants could have prepared the drink to be shown on screen. Could there be someone else on the staff with a grudge against Gabe — a grudge strong enough to result in murder? But black snakeroot wasn't common or particularly easy to find, especially for someone who didn't know what they were looking for. In that case, why would the plant be the weapon of choice for a member of the crew? Unfortunately, that line of questioning brought the focus right back around to Georgine — and, Kaylee realized with a jolt, to Holly Sampson, who had provided the vegetables in the first place.

"May I have that lab report, Giles?" Nick asked after a few moments of silence in the room. Kaylee peered at him, but couldn't read his expression. "I'd better take it to the sheriff ASAP. It seems we're officially looking for a murderer."

The weekend passed slowly for Kaylee. The Flower Patch experienced its usual warm-weather bustle on Saturday, which kept her and Mary busy, but after closing time, Kaylee found herself at a loss. Reese was working long hours at the farm to get it ready for the upcoming wedding, so she didn't have the pleasure of his company to distract her from contemplating the details of Gabe's murder. Without a peep from the sheriff's department about the matter, Kaylee was on pins and needles, worried that one of her friends or a fellow plant enthusiast could be responsible.

Kaylee filled her time by going on long walks with Bear, attending Sunday morning church service, and accomplishing a few odd tasks around Wildflower Cottage, but all the while she was troubled by the case—and troubled by the fact that she had no idea what her next move ought to be. How could she prove Vanessa, Georgine, and Holly innocent? The best way to exonerate them would be to zero in on other potential killers. But who? The most obvious suspects were Gabe's colleagues at *Restaurant Restarts*.

Fortunately, an appointment Kaylee had scheduled for first thing Monday morning gave her an opportunity to explore the theory. Leaving a disappointed Bear at the shop, she and Mary set out for Madrona Grove in the shop's delivery van, carting mock-up bouquets and sketches to show Josh Rutherford and Savannah Ott, the young couple who would be getting married at the farm later that week—if all went as planned.

"I know you're not a big fan of the show's smoke and mirrors," Kaylee said to Mary as she drove down the scenic byway that led from Turtle Cove to the farm, "but I'm grateful you're willing to take the lead for the filming of this segment. I can't say I felt particularly comfortable when they had me talk to Vanessa on camera in the garden the other day."

"Being filmed doesn't bother me. Every one of my dispatch calls was recorded." Mary had been a police dispatcher for many years before retirement led her to a second career as a floral designer. "Besides, we've already gone over the ideas with Josh and Savannah. This is just for show."

"Hopefully it goes as smoothly the second time." Kaylee couldn't help but be suspicious that Sawyer and Garth would try to orchestrate some sort of drama during the meeting, but she hoped she was wrong. Although they'd seemed intent on stirring up trouble at dinner with Reese the other night—especially with their veiled threats against The Flower Patch and Death by Chocolate—they hadn't mentioned firing Kaylee or Jessica since. With luck, the showrunners had truly decided to put the focus on love triumphing over tragedy as Sawyer had said.

"Have you given more thought to who might have given Gabe that snakeroot bulb?" Mary's question broke through Kaylee's thoughts. "I admit, I've been wondering about it since you filled me in Friday."

"I've given it plenty of thought, but I haven't gotten anywhere," Kaylee answered. "I'm hoping that somebody on the crew can shed some light on it for me."

The first crew member Kaylee had the chance to discuss Gabe's death with was Suzy the makeup artist. It proved to be an easy conversation to spark, as Suzy clearly relished gossiping about the topic.

"How has morale been on the set since Gabe died?" Kaylee asked as she sat in a director's chair in the makeup trailer and Suzy began sponging foundation on her face.

Suzy's lips quirked into a brief, cynical smirk, then she put on a more serious expression. "We're all sad, of course, but the show must go on. Granted, the show seems to be going on a bit smoother than before without Gabe trying to dictate everything to everyone."

"Did he rub a lot of people the wrong way?" Kaylee asked, feigning ignorance of the host's difficult behavior on set.

Suzy gave an exaggerated eye roll as she brushed blush onto Kaylee's cheeks. "Who didn't he irritate?" She set the brush onto her cart, then ticked off her fingers. "Vanessa, obviously. And Garth couldn't stand it when Gabe was always calling cues. And Nino wanted to deck him every time he complained about the sun being in his eyes. I even heard that Gabe and that cute carpenter had a big fight over some girl."

Kaylee would have narrowed her eyes, but Suzy had pulled out a mascara brush and ordered her to open them wider.

"You mean Reese?" Mary asked sweetly. "That's Kaylee's boyfriend."

Suzy paused briefly, then resumed smoothly sweeping on the black liquid. "Are you the one they were fighting over?"

"Not to my knowledge," Kaylee said uncomfortably.

"That's a surprise. Dark hair, nice figure—you're definitely Gabe's type." Suzy tilted her head and scrutinized Kaylee's face. "Maybe a little too old, though. No offense."

"None taken," Kaylee replied. "What about you? Didn't you have problems with Gabe's demands?" *Okay, maybe a little offense taken.*

Suzy barked a laugh and adjusted her trendy glasses. "None that I haven't had with a million other prima donnas." She examined Kaylee's face again, then pronounced, "You're good to go."

"My turn, I guess," Mary said, swapping places with Kaylee.

"Oh my goodness!" Suzy squealed as she examined Mary. "Your skin is flawless. What kind of moisturizer do you use?"

From there, the conversation drifted to other topics—mostly skin care—and Kaylee didn't learn much more about anyone on the show's staff. A short while later, a freshly made-up Kaylee and Mary stood just outside the barn with Josh, a handsome young man with sandy-brown hair and square-framed glasses, and his bride-to-be, Savannah, a petite blonde with delicate features and a sunny smile. Mary's eyes twinkled as she showed the couple some of the sketches in her notebook.

"Because the ceremony is in the orchard and the reception will take place in a barn, I chose white daisies as the main flower in the bouquets," Mary said.

"Those are my favorite flowers," Savannah gushed. "I used to make daisy-chain crowns when I was a little girl and pretend I was a princess."

"And now you're going to have a wedding fit for a princess," Josh said, beaming at his fiancée. "Or should I say a cowgirl?"

Savannah turned wide, eager eyes on Mary. "Do you think you could make me a daisy crown to wear with my dress?"

Kaylee held back a smile. Matching daisy crowns for Savannah and her flower girl were already part of the plan, so she knew the bride-to-be was playing up the request for the sake of on-camera excitement. She flicked a glance at Sawyer, who stood behind the camera with Garth and Nino. Based on the producer's smug expression, he was pleased with Savannah's acting.

"I think that's a wonderful idea," Mary agreed. "And, in keeping with the country wedding theme, the decor will also feature barrels cut in half with floral arrangements floating in them." She gestured to some empty halved barrels resting in front of them.

"Floating on water?" Savannah clarified, though this too was also for the sake of the audience. "That sounds interesting, doesn't it, honey? Floating flower gardens? I never knew there was such a thing."

"They will certainly be unique," Mary said. "And Kaylee will be sharing some very special plants that will really elevate the whole look. Right, Kaylee?"

Kaylee froze momentarily, then smiled. "Yes, *Hygrophila difformis* will provide a green, wispy addition to the arrangements."

The couple wore the same confused expression. "What kind of plant is that?" Josh asked. "And how do you say it again?"

Kaylee grimaced. "Sorry. It's called water wisteria. It's got feathery leaves, but more important than its beauty is that it's an oxygenated plant, which means it keeps water clean."

"Great idea, Kaylee," Mary said. "The clean water will reflect the light and brighten that big, dark barn even more."

"I'm so excited," Savannah said, her voice like a bell.

"I'm glad." Mary smiled at the bride, then continued talking about the barrel decorations. "There will be at least twenty barrels. Our carpenter, Reese, has already started cutting them, as you can see." She indicated the halved barrels again. "We'll put a couple at each entrance and more around the dance floor."

"What other flowers are you including?" Josh asked.

"We'll add pickerelweed for a splash of color," Mary answered. "It's long-stemmed with spikes of blue-purple flowers, and it grows in water, so it'll look natural in the barrels."

"That'll match the bridesmaids' dresses," Savannah chimed in.

Mary nodded. "And I'll add a few bluish-purple flowers to the bouquets to pull the whole picture together. I'm leaning toward delphinium."

"Sounds great to me, but what do I know?" Josh shared a laugh with his bride-to-be and touched her hand fondly. "I'll let this be your department, honey." The pair locked starry-eyed gazes on each other and Savannah giggled, flushing a pretty pink.

"Actually, I think we should let this be The Flower Patch's department," she said, shooting a smile at Mary and Kaylee.

Then she grew more somber. "I'm just so, so grateful we can move forward despite the tragic loss of Gabe Forester. Josh and I want to dedicate our wedding to him, to remind us all that love can triumph in the face of tragedy." Savannah held Josh's gaze for a few moments before the scene wrapped.

"Cut!" Garth called.

Sawyer rushed forward. "That was great, everyone. Savannah, you really sold me on your reaction to the plans. And you nailed that last bit about Gabe."

"I minored in theater when I was getting my marketing degree," the young woman said. "I hadn't realized how close the two things could be tied together until now."

"You never cease to amaze me," Josh told his bride.

Although she wasn't wild about the fact that Sawyer had obviously coached Savannah's reactions, Kaylee nevertheless felt a wave of happiness for the couple. They were clearly head over heels for each other, and she was glad to have even a small part in the most important day of their lives.

"That could be you someday," Mary murmured, nudging Kaylee in the ribs gently.

Kaylee scoffed, though she experienced another jolt of joy at the mental picture of her and Reese choosing flower arrangements. Shaking her head, she said, "I thought you were done meddling now that we're dating."

"Where's the fun in that?" Mary's blue eyes twinkled.

Sawyer clapped his hands. "That's all we need from Mary and Katie. Josh and Savannah, we're going to film Matt showing you your ceremony location out in the orchard next, then you'll come back to the barn kitchen for your food tasting with Vanessa. Got it?"

The couple agreed, then followed Sawyer and Garth away from the barn. A few other crew members, including Nino, lingered around the flower consultation set, but they didn't seem to be paying Mary and Kaylee any mind.

"That wasn't too painful," Mary said cheerily as she tucked her notebook under her arm.

Kaylee nodded enthusiastically. "Much better than my chat with Vanessa in the garden."

Movement in the parking area caught Kaylee's eye, and she saw Holly's van pulling into an empty space. Holly emerged toting a large bushel basket of vegetables, which she carried over to where Kaylee and Mary stood.

After exchanging greetings, Kaylee tapped the basket. "Are you making another delivery?"

"Yup," Holly said. "Vanessa ordered baby spinach, tomatoes, basil, and garlic, so I have a hunch Caprese salad is on the wedding menu."

Mary hummed appreciatively. "That'd be a good use of the fresh mozzarella from the cows."

Kaylee's stomach rumbled at the mention of food. She had been too nervous about filming the segment to eat breakfast. Her appetite vanished, however, when she remembered that the last time she'd run into Holly at Madrona Grove had been on the day Gabe died. She wondered if the sheriff's department had talked to Holly about the deliveries she'd made to the farm, so she asked her friend as much.

"They came by yesterday," Holly said. "Apparently dating a deputy doesn't excuse me from police interviews." She and one of the youngest deputies on the force, Alan Brooks, had been romantically linked since she'd moved to the island permanently. "Alan gave me a heads-up that they were sending Robyn to talk to me about the delivery I made that day. It was still nerve-racking, even though I didn't do anything wrong."

Kaylee grimaced sympathetically. "What did Robyn ask you?"

"Mostly about what was in the order, which was just fruits and vegetables." Holly knit her brow. "She asked a lot about onions—whether any were in there, what kind they were, that sort of thing."

"And did you bring Vanessa onions from your greenhouse?" Kaylee asked.

"Yes, red ones," Holly answered.

"Any pearl onions?"

"Nope."

"Anything that looked like a bulb?"

"You sound an awful lot like Robyn." Holly set her basket down on the ground. "You were there with me that day. We gave her the baskets, and she took each thing out and set it on the counter. Did you see anything that looked like a plant bulb?"

Kaylee's mind replayed the memory of Vanessa unpacking the baskets, removing carrots, cucumbers, peppers, tomatoes, celery, and red onions. Nothing that resembled a snakeroot bulb. "No I didn't." She gave her friend an apologetic smile. "I didn't mean to give you the third degree. I'm just baffled and trying to find some clarity."

"I figured you were on the case." Holly winked. "Why all the interest in plant bulbs? Alan couldn't tell me. He said they're being pretty tight-lipped about the investigation since Gabe was a celebrity. They don't want the tabloids getting their hands on the story before they know what happened. Otherwise people will make up all kinds of stories."

"Speaking of being a celebrity, I saw a short blurb on the news about his death, but nothing else," Mary said. "I'd have thought Jocko McGee would come sniffing around here as soon as the coroner's van showed up."

"No kidding," Holly agreed. She'd once been the victim of Jocko's poorly researched writing and wasn't a fan of the fame-hungry reporter. "But his absence is probably a relief for Vanessa."

Mary nudged Kaylee. "Tell her what Giles found."

"Apparently the coroner discovered a black snakeroot bulb in Gabe's stomach," Kaylee said. "It resembled a pearl onion."

"The killer garnished his drink with it," Mary added conspiratorially. "If you can believe that."

Holly's gaze scanned the barnyard, which was still full of various filming equipment and trailers. "Honestly, I *can* believe it. I don't think there's any aspect of this circus that isn't done for dramatic effect, or is actually what it seems." She sighed. "Speaking of things that aren't what they seem, I'd better get these vegetables to Vanessa so she can pretend for the camera that she grew them."

"I'd be happy to deliver those for you." At the sound of Reese's voice, Kaylee felt a rush of warmth. She whirled around to see him approaching from behind the barn, his tool belt buckled around his waist. He hugged her, then left his arm around her shoulders as he nodded to Mary and Holly. "Good morning, ladies. How was filming?"

"I think it went well," Mary answered. "That young couple is as cute as a button."

Reese nodded. "Their enthusiasm is contagious. I notice a change in morale every time they're visiting the farm."

"I'm sure morale could use a boost around here," Holly said. "Reese, were you serious about taking these veggies to Vanessa? That'd be a huge help. I've got a few more deliveries to make."

"No problem. I'm headed to the kitchen now anyway to fix an issue with the plumbing." He glanced down at Kaylee. "Can I interest you in a tour of the barn? A lot has changed since you saw it last week."

"I'd love it," Kaylee said, then grimaced. "But Mary and I

really ought to get back to the shop. We're due to open soon, and Bear is alone."

Mary waved dismissively. "Don't be silly. I'll take the delivery van back to the shop and open up."

"And I'll drive you to town in a little bit," Reese added. "I was going to ask you to lunch anyway."

Touched by the kindness her friends all showed each other and her, Kaylee beamed at Mary and Holly, then finally at Reese. "Well in that case, I'd love a tour."

10

While Mary and Holly set off for the parking area, Reese carried the bushel basket of produce as he led Kaylee along a freshly laid cobblestone path to the barn's main entrance.

"These are new," Kaylee said, indicating the double wooden doors featuring beveled glass with *Madrona Grove* etched on them in a classic script. Since Reese's hands were full, she depressed the lever on the brass handle and opened the door for him.

"Just put them in about midnight last night." Reese entered the barn with Kaylee close behind.

"You were here that late?" Kaylee shook her head. "You've really put your all into this project." As her eyes adjusted to the dim interior, she saw just how right she was about Reese's dedication to the farm's renovation. The barn's interior—once a dusty, weather-beaten space full of cobwebs and splintered wood—was nothing short of stunning.

Freshly polished hardwood floors gleamed in the sunlight streaming through the new windows. Glancing up, she saw how the hammered-iron light fixtures hanging from the rafters would enhance the floor's glow even more when they were illuminated. Against the nearest wall, handcrafted shelving stood behind a rustic barnwood counter with a glass bakery case embedded in it. Beyond the counter, where once there had been a rickety barn ladder, Reese and his crew had built a staircase that led to the former hayloft, which stretched the length of the barn and would serve as more seating space. The space beneath the loft had been enclosed, creating room for Vanessa's kitchen on one end of the barn and sealing off the milking area from the restaurant on the other end. The milking area was only accessible from the outside and would soon be moved to the new cowshed, which was near completion. Vanessa had mentioned that she hoped to eventually replace the milking stalls with a retail shop.

Kaylee stood gazing at the room, awestruck by the transformation. "Reese, this is amazing."

"We're supposed to take delivery of custom tables and chairs tomorrow," he explained. "And since this is a restaurant, safety is key, so they're all coated with the same fire-resistant varnish as the floor."

"Hopefully Sawyer forgets to make you paint them yellow," Kaylee joked.

Reese chuckled, then went on. "We also installed a sprinkler system, and there are fire extinguisher cabinets built into the walls, so everything is up to code." He nodded toward the stairs. "I'd take you up to the loft, but we don't have the railing put in yet. I think once it's done, it'll be my favorite spot. You can see the whole first floor from up there."

"I'm sure it's incredible, just like everything else." Kaylee walked a few steps toward the counter and ran her fingers along the stainless steel surface, which contrasted the barnwood base to great effect. "I can't believe you did all this."

"I didn't do it alone." Reese's tone was modest, but Kaylee detected the sense of pride he felt at a job well done.

"No, but you oversaw it all." She returned to Reese's side and planted a kiss on his cheek. "I knew you were capable of this sort of thing, but to see it with my own eyes makes it even more special." She beamed. "I'm so proud of you."

"Thank you, Kaylee. That means a lot." Even in the dim, she could see Reese's face redden, likely with a mix of embarrassment and appreciation. He lifted the basket slightly. "Want to see the kitchen?"

Kaylee nodded enthusiastically. "Lead the way."

The sound of 1980s pop music grew louder as they crossed the cavernous dining room toward a swinging door at the back. Reese used his shoulder to nudge the door open, and Kaylee followed him inside, where they found Vanessa with her back to them, holding the lid on a blender as the appliance whirred.

Kaylee took a moment to appreciate the professional kitchen. The modern amenities were in stark contrast to the rustic dining area, but no less impressive. Stainless steel appliances—including two oversize ovens, dual cooktops, and a massive walk-in refrigerator—rested against the tiled walls. Brand-new copper pots and pans hung from a rack installed over the metal work space set in the center of the room, and anti-fatigue mats dotted the classic black-and-white tile floor. Wooden utensils in stoneware crocks, butcher-block cutting boards, and wire baskets toting potatoes and onions added a homey element to the metal fixtures.

The blender churned loudly over the music, and Vanessa swayed to the peppy song. Kaylee thought her new friend appeared right at home, filled with happiness in her dream kitchen. But with a lurch, Kaylee remembered that Vanessa was likely one of the sheriff's prime suspects in Gabe's murder. *Please let them be wrong about her.*

Reese set the bushel of vegetables on the counter with a thud, and Vanessa jolted, releasing her hold on the blender's power button. The machine went silent in an instant, though the stereo continued to play.

"You scared me." Vanessa laughed stiffly. "I didn't hear you come in."

"Sorry to startle you, but I come bearing gifts," Reese said. "Holly dropped these off."

"And Reese offered to give me a tour," Kaylee added. "The place looks amazing."

Vanessa glanced around with awe-filled eyes. "I keep thinking I'm dreaming. It's all so perfect. Thanks to you, Reese."

"I'm not the one to thank," Reese said. "You and Matt were the ones who came up with the design."

Something approaching regret flickered in Vanessa's eyes, then she blinked and nodded to the blender, which contained a reddish liquid. "Do you guys want some Veggie Vigor juice? This batch is spoken for, but I could whip up another one."

"No thanks," Reese answered, pulling a wrench from his tool belt. "I'm just going to readjust the sink pipes a little to get you better water pressure."

"You're a lifesaver," Vanessa said as Reese dropped beneath the industrial sink. "What about you, Kaylee?"

Kaylee studied the blender pitcher and did her best not to cringe. "It certainly looks interesting."

Vanessa laughed as she poured a generous helping into a glass. "That's a nice way to put it. It might not appear particularly appetizing, but it sure does get the job done. And fast."

Kaylee frowned, wondering at Vanessa's statement. She couldn't possibly mean that it had done the job of killing Gabe, could she? "What's in it?"

"Cucumber, tomatoes, apples, herbs, and a few other special ingredients."

"Any onions?" Kaylee hated that Vanessa had sparked doubt in her, but she couldn't help but ask.

"Just a little. Nothing too overpowering, I promise." Vanessa walked to the bushel basket, then peered inside and grinned. "This all looks fantastic. I hope we're able to grow produce anywhere near as delicious as Holly's."

Footsteps thudded across the dining room, growing louder by the moment until the kitchen door swung wide and Sawyer appeared.

"Nino and his crew are on their way in here to set up for the tasting," the producer announced, then frowned at Vanessa, who was unpacking the basket. "Why don't you have anything plated yet?"

Vanessa's lightness disappeared. "I just received my delivery. Besides, I was making the juice you asked for."

Sawyer checked his watch, not masking his irritation, then grabbed the glass Vanessa had set on the counter. "Well at least you got one thing right." He took a huge swig, then put the glass down. "I don't care what Gabe said, these are delicious."

"And so good for you too. Right, Sawyer?" The chill in Vanessa's tone alarmed Kaylee.

"Yup," Sawyer said, clearly oblivious to Vanessa's growing coldness. He picked up an eggplant that Vanessa had just unpacked and tossed it from hand to hand. "Say, Vanessa, I've been meaning to ask you—what do you think about adding a third dinner option for the wedding reception? Maybe some seafood? Chicken and steak are so . . . pedestrian."

"We already settled on the menu, Sawyer." Vanessa's jaw was clenched so tight that her words barely made it out.

Reese reappeared from beneath the sink, tucking his wrench back into his tool belt. "I'm all done here, Vanessa. You're good to go."

"Thanks, Reese. I appreciate how you make my work in here easier instead of harder." Vanessa's steely gaze stayed on Sawyer, but he was oblivious, his focus on pretending the eggplant was a basketball.

"Ready?" Reese asked Kaylee, who nodded eagerly. She was excited to spend some time with him, even just a quick lunch, after barely seeing him recently.

"I'll walk out with you, Reese," Sawyer said, dunking the eggplant in the bushel basket with a flourish. "I wanted to talk to you about something."

A flicker of annoyance flashed across Reese's face, but Kaylee figured that she was likely the only one in the room who caught it, and only because she knew him so well. Even easygoing Reese seemed to be irritated by the prickly producer.

"Ugh!" Vanessa held up a crumpled bouquet of herbs. "Sawyer smooshed the basil I needed for garnish. Kaylee, do you think the basil you planted last week is healthy enough to pick from?"

"Should be," Kaylee said. "Enough for today, anyway, assuming you're only doing a couple of salads."

"Okay, good."

Vanessa grabbed a pair of kitchen shears, and then she and Kaylee followed the men out of the kitchen just as Nino and a couple of other crew members were coming through toward them, laden with equipment. Nino nodded a greeting to Kaylee and Vanessa, his face smug, and Kaylee wondered if there was a particular reason for his smugness or if that was just his personality.

"So tell me, Reese," Sawyer was saying as they crossed the dining room, "do you think we could skip the railing on the upstairs dining area? It would really be in the way of getting a clear shot at the wedding reception. We want to be able to see the guests' faces. Right, Nino?"

"Right, boss," Nino agreed, though he continued on toward the kitchen without stopping to discuss the matter. Kaylee got the impression that he said that phrase a lot, whether he meant it or not.

"So what do you think?" Sawyer asked Reese eagerly.

Reese shook his head. "It's not safe to have diners up there without a railing. That's a twelve-foot drop."

"Got it." Sawyer snapped his fingers and pointed at Reese. "Safety first. But do me a favor and think on it. I mean, hopefully people are smart enough to stay away from the edge of the loft, right?"

Kaylee and Vanessa exchanged glances. Vanessa rolled her eyes and mouthed, "Typical."

Sawyer pushed through the barn's new front door, followed by Reese, who held the door for Kaylee and Vanessa. They almost walked straight into Sawyer, however, who had stopped short on the sidewalk.

"What's that woman doing here?" he muttered, then strode purposefully toward a white Mercedes parked a few yards away.

Standing near the sleek luxury car were Georgine Snowbird and a well-dressed, middle-aged man Kaylee didn't recognize. Wondering who he was, she followed Sawyer, with Reese and Vanessa right behind her.

"What are you doing here?" Sawyer repeated, shaking a finger at Georgine. A few beads of sweat on his forehead glistened in the sun. "You have no right to be here."

"You don't own this property." Georgine jerked a thumb toward Vanessa. "She does."

Sawyer swiped at his brow and glared at Georgine but said nothing more before he retreated into the barn.

"You're Vanessa Vanguard?" the mystery visitor asked. He extended a hand, and Kaylee saw the glint of a ruby ring on his pinky. "Erwin Blackstock."

Vanessa frowned, but shook his hand anyway. "What can I do for you, Mr. Blackstock?"

"From what I hear, it's what I can do for you," Erwin said. "Rumor has it you're not happy with your purchase."

"How is that your concern?" Vanessa's tone was justifiably wary, and Reese and Kaylee glanced at each other with similar skepticism in their eyes.

"I bid on this property when it went up for auction, just like you. Due to a computer glitch, my highest bid didn't go through, and you and your husband beat me out of a heck of a good deal." Erwin straightened his wide, gold tie. "I'm here to right that wrong, if you will."

Vanessa's eyebrows shot up. "You want to buy the farm?"

"Considering the work that's gone into it, I'd be willing to give you what you paid." Erwin smiled arrogantly.

"Well, Mr. Blackstock, that's very generous," Vanessa said politely. "But the answer is no."

Kaylee would have thought that Vanessa would jump at the chance to unload the farm, but maybe she was holding out for a better offer.

"What if I give you what you paid plus ten percent?" Erwin asked.

"No." Vanessa stood ramrod straight, her fingers clenched around the kitchen shears still in her hand. "My husband and I are making our dream a reality here. We've poured blood, sweat, and tears into this place, and no amount of money will convince us to walk away from it."

"Ms. Snowbird here tells me it's cursed." Acidity edged into Erwin's voice. "It'd be a shame to open your little restaurant and have nobody show up because they're scared. Not to mention the murder that took place here."

Her eyes hardening, Vanessa said, "If you believe Madrona Grove is cursed, then I don't know why you'd want it anyway. Good day, Mr. Blackstock. Please remove yourself from my property."

Vanessa spun on her heel and strode back into the barn, leaving everyone in the barnyard speechless for a moment. Kaylee was proud of her friend for standing her ground, though she felt bad that Vanessa had clearly forgotten she'd come outside to snip some basil. As she watched the door bang shut behind Vanessa, Kaylee saw that Sawyer had returned, this time with Nino—and his camera—in tow. They must have been there for most of the exchange between Vanessa and Erwin because Sawyer was grinning, clearly thrilled at the scene his cameraman had just captured on film.

Kaylee grimaced as though she had tasted rotten fruit. *What is it with these guys?* Then she squinted at Sawyer and saw that he was still sweating. Was it the warm sun, or was he ill?

Before she could contemplate it further, Kaylee's thoughts were interrupted by a piercing shriek — the scream of someone in immense pain.

11

Another shout came from the pasture, and Kaylee and Reese took off for the cow enclosure, only to be accompanied by Nino with his camera on his shoulder. Whatever happened would be documented. *But is it real?*

Kaylee shook off the thought and focused on locating the source of the scream. Reese hurriedly unlatched the pasture gate, and they saw Matt on the ground at the far end, writhing in pain and gripping his lower leg.

"It bit me!" he hollered, his reddened face contorted in agony. "A snake. I didn't see it until it was too late." He let out a wail. "I don't know what kind it was. I don't know if it's venomous or not."

"We don't have any venomous snakes on Orcas," Reese said reassuringly as he searched the grass around Matt. "None that are native, anyway."

"Just to be safe, I'll call for an ambulance." Kaylee pulled her cell phone out of her pocket. She quickly dialed and relayed the situation to the dispatcher, who told her an ambulance was on its way, then instructed Kaylee to hold for directions on how to help Matt. While she waited for the operator to come back on the line, she noticed that Sawyor, Garth, and several other people had come to the pasture—though whether it was to help Matt or merely to revel in the drama, she wasn't sure.

At Garth's silent direction, Nino had edged close to Matt and was filming the distraught farmer. The idea that Sawyer and his crew would use this frightening incident to benefit the show turned her stomach.

"Ma'am," the dispatcher said, "can you ask if the patient saw the snake's coloring?"

Kaylee hurried closer to Matt, who appeared to be calming down though still in shock, and repeated the question.

Matt nodded. "There were stripes, like a coral snake. That's all I saw before it bit me and disappeared in the grass. I didn't even see it approach me. I think I might have stepped on it, but I'm not sure."

After Kaylee relayed the information to the dispatcher, the operator said, "Keep his leg below his heart level. If there's any venom, it will move through the body slower that way."

Kaylee called out the instructions to Reese, who was now beside Matt.

"You can wash the area lightly with a cleansing wipe," the dispatcher instructed, "but don't put anything on it."

"Okay, thank you." Kaylee heard a siren in the distance, and she scanned the horizon for flashing lights. "The ambulance is almost here."

When Kaylee turned back to Matt, she saw that Georgine had pushed through the bystanders and knelt down beside him. She was applying something to his leg.

Kaylee rushed forward to stop her. "Don't put anything on the snakebite. The dispatcher said only to clean it gently."

Georgine nodded solemnly but didn't stop. "The dispatcher would be correct, but they don't know about the ways of my people. We have remedies for snakebites. If there is any venom, it will be drawn out with this."

"What is it?" Sawyer asked, waving for Nino to angle the camera toward Georgine.

"It's a remedy passed down from my ancestors," the herbalist replied.

"You mean the ones who cursed this land?" Sawyer asked.

Before Georgine could answer, Vanessa burst into the cow pasture, fear plain on her face. "Matt!" she cried as she ran straight for her husband and fell to his side, enfolding him in her arms. Georgine stood up and edged away from the couple, as did Reese.

"Vanessa," Matt said, his breathing ragged. "I have to tell you something."

"Shh." Vanessa brushed fingertips across his blanched face. "Everything will be fine. You'll see."

"No, listen to me." Matt grabbed the back of his wife's neck and pulled her close so their foreheads touched. "I am so sorry. Everything has been my fault, and if I could undo it all I would."

"I love it here, Matt. I do." Vanessa bit back a sob. "Please don't do this to yourself. Just focus on getting better. That's all I want."

Matt shook his head. "But that's not all you want. You wanted a baby of our own. You wanted a family."

"I have you. You're all the family I need."

Kaylee felt a warm presence, and she realized that Reese was now by her side. He grasped her hand, and she drew strength from his touch as they waited for the ambulance.

Tears escaped from Matt's eyes. "I shouldn't have signed us up for the show, but I was desperate. I wanted to make it work so badly . . ." Matt trailed off, guilt washing over his face.

"You wanted to give me my dream. That's why you were willing to do anything."

"It was irresponsible of me."

"No, Matt, you were trying to make me happy. You knew this farm and restaurant were what I always dreamed of."

"You dreamed of a baby."

Vanessa smiled. "I dreamed of a family on a farm. I have my farm, and I have my family. You're my family, Matt."

Kaylee felt tears well in her eyes, and she blinked them back. Of all the things she had seen on the set of *Restaurant Restarts*, the touching scene she'd just witnessed between Vanessa and Matt was the most genuine.

At least it appeared to be.

Considering the camera Nino had aimed at the couple for the duration of their emotional exchange, Kaylee couldn't be too sure.

Kaylee's familiar fears about the show's lack of authenticity resurfaced as she and Reese arrived at the Orcas Island Medical Center to support Vanessa and check up on Matt. The *Restaurant Restarts* mobile filming van was parked right in front of the emergency room door. Several crew members were milling about, including the ubiquitous trio of Garth, Sawyer, and Nino.

Just beyond the men, who were huddled deep in conversation, she caught sight of an unlikely duo facing off beside the sliding glass entry doors—Georgine and Nick. The herbalist stood proud and straight, her chin lifted defiantly.

"Why don't I drop you off and go park?" Reese asked. He nodded toward Nick, who was waving at them. "I'm guessing you're the one he wants to talk to."

Kaylee flashed Reese a smile. "Thanks. I'll wait for you by the doors." She hopped out of Reese's black pickup, then passed the showrunners and approached Nick and Georgine.

"Kaylee, I'm glad you're here," Nick said.

"What can I do for you?" she asked.

"Maybe you can help us settle a dispute we're having. It's about a certain plant called snakeroot, which Ms. Snowbird applied to Matt Vanguard's snakebite just now. I say it's poisonous—deadly, as we all know—but Ms. Snowbird says it has medicinal qualities. Is that true?"

Kaylee thought immediately of the of the black snakeroot bulb that had killed Gabe. "Some varieties are deadly, yes. But snakeroot is a common name for more than one plant. There's the lily derivative that killed Gabe, but there's also the aster derivative called white snakeroot that can poison cows. And then there's one called black cohosh, which has been used historically for treating certain maladies like snakebites and . . ." She glanced at Georgine, who had a knowing glint in her eyes.

"And what?" Nick raised an eyebrow. "Were you going to say infertility?"

"You knew about Vanessa's inability to have a baby, didn't you?" Kaylee asked Georgine.

"I overheard them speaking about it one morning at the beginning of filming," Georgine answered. "I thought perhaps if they had a child, they would be willing to give up this farm before the curse claims another victim. I offered to help."

Nick crossed his arms. "Ms. Snowbird claims that she was bringing Matt some snakeroot today because he asked her for it."

"He did," Georgine said. "I mentioned it to him a few days ago, and he asked me to give him some. He wasn't sure when the right time to bring up the idea with his wife would be, so we kept it between us. It's why I was at the farm today. I was delivering the snakeroot he requested."

"And I was just about to ask what other kinds of snakeroot she might have available to her," Nick said. "And who she might have given them to."

Kaylee cringed. It appeared Georgine was back on top of the sheriff's suspect list—not that it was likely they'd ever removed her.

Kaylee's phone chimed, and she checked the screen. Reese had texted. *Lot full, had to park far away. See you in a few.* The sliding doors behind Kaylee opened with a whoosh, and she turned to find Vanessa standing there. The young woman stood frozen for a moment, and soon Nino had a camera in her face.

Trying to ignore Nino, Kaylee went to Vanessa. "How is Matt?"

"He's fine. No snake venom was found in his system," Vanessa replied with a gracious smile. Then her expression frosted over. "The doctors are baffled, though, because there are no aggressive snakes native to Orcas Island." Vanessa stared straight at the camera then, though Kaylee wondered if she was gazing past the lens to Sawyer. "It's very suspicious that Matt was bitten on our farm, actually."

"What a relief that he'll be okay." Kaylee pulled Vanessa into a hug. "I'm glad the snake didn't poison him."

Vanessa stiffened and backed out of Kaylee's embrace. She shot a glare toward the TV van. "The snake didn't harm my husband, but that doesn't mean he's safe."

12

The chef spun on her heel and strode back into the hospital.

"Oh man, that was gold!" Sawyer exclaimed. "You caught all that, right, Nino?"

"Sure thing, boss." The cameraman made eye contact with Kaylee briefly, then carried his equipment to the back of the van.

Just as Nino disappeared behind the vehicle, Reese appeared from the parking lot. He waved to Kaylee and jogged over to where she stood on the sidewalk. "Sorry it took so long. I had to park all the way at the back of the lot." He jabbed a thumb toward the TV van. "Looks like you weren't bored."

Kaylee was about to respond when Sawyer interrupted. "Hey, Katie. I need to talk to you."

"Sawyer, you know her name is Kaylee," Reese said, aggravation edging his voice.

"Right, right." The producer nodded, though there was a touch of condescension in his tone. "Anyway, can you come back to the farm and film some more scenes in the garden tomorrow morning?"

Kaylee knit her brow. "Didn't you get enough footage of me and Vanessa last week?"

Sawyer shrugged. "There are a few more, ah, botany-related questions I'd like you to answer on camera. Talk about the vegetables and whatever. Our housewife viewers really eat that stuff up."

"I don't know," Kaylee said hesitantly. "I don't feel that comfortable on camera."

"That's too bad." Sawyer sniffed. "The Vanguards could

really use more . . . uplifting footage going into this show. So much of what we've shot has been a bummer."

"What are you getting at, Sawyer?" Reese asked, gravel in his tone.

The producer shrugged. "You guys seem pretty tight with Matt and Vanessa. I'm sure you'd hate for their success to be endangered by a negative portrayal on *Restaurant Restarts*."

"But you're in charge of how they're portrayed," Kaylee started to protest, then instantly understood what the sleazy producer was saying. "Oh. I see."

"I knew you would. Garth, come over here." Sawyer snapped his fingers, and the director joined them swiftly. "Kaylee is coming back to the farm tomorrow to go over some more plant stuff. Why don't you prep her on what we're expecting?" Sawyer gazed appraisingly at Kaylee. "I'm sure she'll be completely cooperative."

As the producer sauntered off, a flummoxed Kaylee found a silver lining to his threats and insinuations—at least he'd finally gotten her name right.

"Order up for Katie." The clerk behind the counter at Pacific Street Diner pushed a large white paper bag across the counter. "Is there a Katie here?"

"Very funny." Kaylee gave Reese a playful shove as he collected the sack of takeout they were bringing to The Flower Patch to share with Mary. "I'm surprised Sawyer doesn't call you Ross."

"Well, he is signing my paychecks," Reese said, guiding Kaylee toward the door and holding it open for her with his free hand. "Supposed to be, anyway."

"You haven't been paid yet?" Kaylee thought the showrunners couldn't surprise her any more than they already had with their underhanded tactics. If they weren't paying their workers, then she had been wrong.

"They gave me a deposit at the outset, and they'll pay the remainder when the project is completed." Reese grasped Kaylee's hand as they turned on Main Street and walked down the sidewalk toward The Flower Patch. It was a beautiful spring day, and after the morning's drama and visit to the hospital, they had agreed they could both use some fresh air—somewhere other than at Madrona Grove.

"I hope they follow through," Kaylee said, somewhat to herself. "I trust them all about as far as I can throw them. And I haven't been to the gym lately."

"What do you think they want you to talk about tomorrow?" Reese asked.

Kaylee shrugged. "Beats me. Garth didn't tell me much." She sighed. "I don't even know why I agreed."

"Because Sawyer threatened the livelihood of someone you care about—again—and you want to do anything you can to help the Vanguards."

"I suppose so. Although . . ." Kaylee hesitated.

"What is it?"

"There's something about Vanessa's behavior. Every time I think she's innocent in all this, that she was thrust into this situation without her consent, she does something that makes me suspect there's more to her than meets the eye."

Reese glanced over at Kaylee, an eyebrow raised. "You think she's the one who killed Gabe?"

"I don't *want* to think that, but I suppose there's always the possibility."

"What about her behavior makes you suspicious?"

"In the restaurant kitchen earlier today, when she was giving that juice to Sawyer, there was a coldness in her that I hadn't sensed before." Kaylee sighed as she recalled the tense scene. "And do you remember how she mentioned something about it 'acting fast'? Now that I think about it, I saw Sawyer sweating outside, just like Gabe did before he died."

"But Sawyer was fine at the hospital. His usual tactless self."

Kaylee laughed drily as they reached The Flower Patch's front porch. "You're right. I'm sure I'm just letting my imagination run away with me."

"Your imagination is part of what makes you good at solving mysteries." Reese squeezed her left hand as she unlatched the front door with her right hand. "It's one of the things I lo—"

Reese's words were cut off by a torrent of barking as a reddish-brown blur rushed through the door and practically jumped into Kaylee's arms.

"My goodness, Bear," Kaylee said, burying her face in his fur as she carried him over the threshold. "I missed you too."

"Are those Pacific Street bacon burgers I smell?" Mary asked from behind the front counter.

"Yes, ma'am." Reese set the bag on the counter. "With extra bacon for Bear."

"I hope he wasn't too much trouble while I was gone," Kaylee said as the little dog lapped at her chin. "I should have taken him on a longer walk this morning."

"He only got excited when he heard you and Reese out front." Mary peeked into the sack. "He's been an angel since I got back from the farm." She raised her eyebrow at Kaylee. "Speaking of the farm, rumor has it there was some excitement after I left."

"You could say that," Kaylee said, sliding a glance toward Reese. "Why don't we put up the Out to Lunch sign? I have a hunch you won't want the story to be interrupted."

"Gosh, Kaylee, where did these awful bags come from?" Suzy grimaced as she scrutinized Kaylee's face in the makeup trailer lights.

Kaylee chose not to take offense at Suzy's typical bluntness. "I didn't sleep very well last night."

"No kidding." Suzy started dabbing concealer under Kaylee's eyes. "What happened? Too much coffee late in the day?"

"Something like that." In fact, Kaylee had made a conscious effort to relax before bed, drinking chamomile tea and snuggling with Bear while reading a classic English novel. But no matter how well she thought she'd set herself up for a restful night, questions continued to surface about the happenings at Madrona Grove, causing her to sleep in fits and starts until she gave up and got out of bed before dawn.

"With your good skin, you're still an easy one." Suzy set aside the concealer, then pumped a glob of foundation onto a sponge and applied it to Kaylee's cheeks.

"It seemed like Gabe might have qualified as a hard one."

Suzy grunted as she grabbed her blush brush. "He always thought he knew my job better than I did, but his suggestions were terrible. I can work a lot of miracles, but the man wasn't twenty-five anymore, you know?"

There was a sharp rap on the trailer door, and Garth entered. "Are you ready for your mic, Kaylee?" He held up a clip-on black microphone with a thin wire that led to a small rectangular box.

With a final swipe of blush, Suzy announced, "She's done." She set down the brush and motioned for Garth to exit. "I'll mic her up outside where there's more room to maneuver."

When Suzy had finished clipping on the microphone, Kaylee walked with Garth a few feet to the cameras set up near the garden. "Do you have any last-minute advice about what I should say?" she asked.

"Sawyer will be there to coach you," Garth said. "Talk about the plants you chose and why. Feel free to explain your reasoning for the plants' placement in the garden."

"Didn't I already do that with Vanessa last week?" Kaylee frowned, then quickly smoothed out her face. She didn't want to mess up Suzy's work.

A flicker of annoyance crossed Garth's face. "We want to be sure we cover all our bases. You know, just in case we need to take a different approach with the show."

"You mean in case Vanessa is arrested for Gabe's murder and you have to edit her out?" Kaylee blurted.

Garth blinked a few times, his face stony. His gaze roamed over the garden, then he finally said, "Our viewers want to learn something when they watch our show. A gardening lesson will entertain them."

"I'm not sure how many of my former students would call my lectures entertaining." Kaylee chuckled, trying to lighten the tension. "I used to be a professor before I moved to Orcas Island. My friends give me a hard time because I still tend to refer to plants by their Latin names, and sometimes I give a little too much information. Take that tomato plant for example." Kaylee pointed out a seedling close to the fence. "Most people would just call it a tomato and move on, but I see *Solanum lycopersicum*, a nightshade species that produces an edible berry. Yes, tomatoes are botanically a berry. They originated in western South America, where the Nahua peoples in that area were already cultivating them by 500 BC. Their word *tomatl* became the Spanish word *tomate*, which we call a tomato in English. See what I mean?"

Garth's eyebrows rose high up his forehead. "Let's just call it a tomato. You lost me at *solara*."

"*Solanum*," Kaylee corrected. "*Solanum lycopersicum* is its scientific name."

"I'll take your word for it." After a dismissive nod to Kaylee, Garth shouted, "Positions, everyone!" His bald head pivoted on his long neck as he scanned the barnyard. "Where's Sawyer?" He grabbed a bullhorn off of a nearby stand. "Sawyer, please report to set."

"Last I heard, he was in his trailer," Suzy called back from near the makeup trailer. "He went in to take a nap earlier. I haven't seen him since."

"A nap?" Garth lifted his bullhorn and called Sawyer's name again.

"Yeah, he said he wasn't feeling well," Suzy said, approaching the garden.

Alarmed, Kaylee asked, "What did he say was wrong?"

Before Suzy answered, a trailer's metal door could be heard slamming shut. "I'm coming!" Sawyer's voice carried to the garden, but it wasn't strong as normal. He sounded weak and tired.

When he appeared from around the side of the barn, his feet faltered a bit. He was breathing heavily, and he was drenched in sweat, his shirt plastered to his chest. He tugged at his collar as he stumbled toward the cameras.

"You can't go on camera looking like that," Garth said. "Suzy, get him some makeup and a new shirt."

"My shirt is fine!" Sawyer yelled. "It's just a little wrinkled. You're supposed to keep the camera on Kaylee anyway."

Kaylee searched Sawyer's pale face. "You don't look well, Sawyer. Are you breathing okay?"

"I'm alive, aren't I?" Irritability layered his response.

Suzy approached with a sport coat and fitted Sawyer's arms through the sleeves. She adjusted the sleeves, then patted his face with some powder.

Sawyer pushed her away. "Enough."

Suzy threw up her hands. "Just what this set needs, another problem child."

"Let's get on with it," Garth said. "Nino, start rolling."

Sawyer and Kaylee stepped into the garden. The producer swiped a coat sleeve across his brow, then said, "Okay, Katie— *Kaylee*, you're here to talk about the wedding flowers."

Kaylee peered at Sawyer. "Actually, I'm here to talk about the vegetables in the garden."

"Vegetables!" Sawyer yelled. "Who wants to listen to you talk about boring vegetables? Are you trying to ruin my show?"

Kaylee turned to Garth for help, but the director twirled his finger to keep going. She cleared her throat and thought quickly. "I suppose I can share about the flowers for the wedding. Again."

"Ugh, bo-ring," Sawyer sneered.

Something is very wrong. "Sawyer, I think you need to see a doctor. You don't look well."

"Just keep talking about the flowers. Or why don't you tell everyone how it feels that your boyfriend and Gabe once came to blows over another woman?" Sawyer stumbled backward. He attempted to catch himself, but with nothing but air around him, he quickly went down, landing in the rich, brown soil.

Despite reeling from the out-of-nowhere mention of Reese and Gabe's long-ago feud, Kaylee dropped to her knees to help him. "How long have you been like this?"

"Been like what?"

"Weak, dizzy, pale, irritable."

"Who are you calling irritable?" Sawyer stared toward the camera. "Is it my insulin, Garth? Is it off?"

"Suzy!" Garth called through his bullhorn. "Get Sawyer something to eat. He's going into shock." Garth lowered the bullhorn and looked at Sawyer. "Do you want me to cut?"

Sawyer shook his head.

When Kaylee realized the camera would continue filming, she wondered why in the world they'd make that call. *Unless this diabetic shock isn't real.*

Frustration grew in Kaylee at once again having to question reality. "Sawyer, are you diabetic?" she asked.

"Usually I'm good about keeping my blood sugar in check." He struggled to stand, his expensive shoes slipping in the dirt. "I hope it's not that juice Vanessa makes me."

Kaylee bit her lip, wondering if she should raise the suggestion that this might not be an insulin problem. These symptoms mimicked Gabe's snakeroot poisoning. If Sawyer had been ingesting the poison slowly over time, rather than a whole bulb at once, the effects might be more drawn out.

Until he dropped dead.

Kaylee placed a gentle hand on his arm. "Sawyer, I think we should get you to the clinic."

"Nonsense. I just need a snack."

"I'm here!" Suzy announced, appearing outside the gate with a granola bar and a glass of red liquid. "I ran into Vanessa and she gave me another juice for you."

Sawyer finally managed to get to his feet. Kaylee tried to support his elbow, but he shrugged her off and stumbled out of the garden toward where Suzy waited.

"Let's take five," Garth called through his megaphone. "Kaylee, I think we'll readjust your position. Can you go stand back in the far corner while we move the cameras? We'll use you to set the lighting."

Although she would have preferred to keep an eye on Sawyer—and find some way to talk him out of drinking the fresh glass of juice—Kaylee did as she was told. She walked carefully through the garden rows, glad to see that all the plants were healthy and that Matt and Vanessa had kept them well watered. Once she'd made her way to the spot Garth had indicated, she alternately cast glances back toward Sawyer and checked the ground for weeds. It was a little early for weeds to pop up since they'd just tilled the garden a few weeks earlier, but she scanned the rows for interloping sprouts anyway.

She saw nothing but healthy seedlings taking root, which gave her a sense of hope that perhaps everything at Madrona Grove was going to be okay after all . . . until she spotted a thin green sprout peeking up from a clump of soil that appeared to have been recently disturbed. She stepped closer to it and crouched down to inspect the small plant. A sinking feeling dragging at her, she scooped soil away from the base and revealed a white bulb with hairy roots that hadn't taken hold yet. She grasped the plant and held it up, her hand shaking slightly.

It was a death camas.

13

Kaylee gazed toward the cameras, where Garth was conversing with Nino. "Do you know what this is?" she asked.

Garth squinted through his glasses at her. "What?"

"Why is there a death camas planted in this garden?" Kaylee's voice was surprisingly steady despite the deadly bulb in her hands.

She heard the soft thud of footsteps behind her, and she glanced over her shoulder to see Sawyer approaching. He appeared less sweaty, but he was still disheveled and pale. He held the juice glass in one hand and twirled his fingers at Garth with the other, a silent command to set the cameras rolling.

"You're filming this too?" Incredulous, Kaylee shook her head. "You planted this here for me to find, didn't you? You wanted to spark some shocked reaction, just like when you brought up Reese and Gabe's past. Do you know how dangerous this plant is?"

"Tell me about how dangerous it is, Kaylee," Sawyer said, his tone at once coaxing and menacing as he crowded close to her. "Better yet, explain for the cameras how you just found the very same plant that killed Gabe planted right here amid the vegetables the Vanguards expect to serve in their restaurant. That sounds to me"—he gazed directly into the closest lens—"like a recipe for disaster."

"Is all of this just fake?" Disgusted, Kaylee flung her arms wide. She accidentally knocked into the glass in Sawyer's hand, sending a cascade of red liquid onto his clothes.

"You clumsy idiot!" Sawyer brushed at his sport coat with his free hand. "You've ruined this whole morning's shoot."

"I'm sorry—"

"You are no longer welcome on this set," Sawyer hissed as he shoved the nearly empty glass into Kaylee's hands. He stalked off through the garden, trampling a few tomato and pepper plants along the way.

Everyone in the vicinity remained intent on their work—or at least remained intent on appearing to work—as Kaylee struggled to make sense of what had just happened. Her heart pounding and her head reeling, she scanned the area for a sympathetic face, but none of the crew members made eye contact.

Finally, she glanced down at the shriveled plant clutched in her hand. The death camas, which had clearly been planted intentionally to get a rise out of her—and was likely the true reason Sawyer had invited her to the farm that morning—indicated that she was right, that nothing was real on the TV set. But Gabe's death *was* real, and, to be honest, Sawyer's bout of sickness certainly would have been difficult to fake too. *He's a master manipulator, but it's not like he can change his skin color at will.*

She shifted her focus to the red liquid streaking the sides and pooling at the bottom of the glass in her other hand. If there was any chance that Vanessa was poisoning Sawyer with her vegetable juice, Kaylee could find out with a simple test in her lab. It was a long shot, but Kaylee knew she would feel better if she could eliminate the possibility that Vanessa was involved in causing trouble on the set of *Restaurant Restarts*.

Clearly, the show's producer was stirring up more than enough on his own.

A short while later, Kaylee stood under a hot shower at Wildflower Cottage, gratefully scrubbing the TV makeup off her face and scouring any last trace of death camas from her hands. She was grateful to have both the bulb and the juice glass safely zipped up in plastic bags. She would have preferred to toss the black snakeroot bulb down the garbage disposal, but considering her wide-ranging suspicions about activity at the farm, she figured it was better to be safe than sorry she'd destroyed evidence—though evidence of what, exactly, she wasn't sure. *Manipulating reality and fabricating drama, at the very least.*

Kaylee continued to mull over the mystery surrounding Gabe's death as she leashed Bear, put the juice glass and plant in her tote, and set out for The Flower Patch, hoping she'd arrive just in time to open for the day. She'd been relying on Mary's generous spirit a lot lately, and she hoped that she could get back to shouldering some of the burden of tourist season at the shop. *Now that I'm essentially banned from the farm, I should have plenty of time*, she thought wryly as she drove along the forested highway that led to Turtle Cove.

Just as she was appreciating the sunlight filtering through the madrone trees and dappling the asphalt, her cell phone rang. She hit the hands-free button on her car's radio to answer. "Hello?"

"I saw what you did." It was a woman's voice, high and raspy.

"What?" Kaylee asked, her heartbeat pounding in her ears.

"Don't mess this up. Do you hear me?"

"Who is this?"

Click.

Kaylee quickly pulled over and retrieved her phone from her pocket to check the caller ID. *Unavailable.*

Kaylee glanced toward her tote, which held the glass and the snakeroot bulb. Is that what the caller had been talking about? Did someone at the farm see her take it? But why would it matter?

Unless someone knew it contained poison. The person who put it there.

Kaylee drove the rest of the way to Turtle Cove in a state of bewilderment. Her daze continued as she parked her SUV behind the shop and let herself and Bear in through the back door. She nearly ran straight into Sheriff Maddox.

"Sheriff!" she exclaimed, putting a hand to her chest as Bear barked a greeting. "What are you doing here?"

A sheepish expression crossed Eddie's face. He nodded toward Mary, who stood at the worktable arranging a bouquet of yellow lilies and purple irises. "Mary is very kindly putting together a bouquet of Susan's favorite flowers for her birthday," he said. "I couldn't remember what they were called, so she let me come back here and pick them out of the cooler."

"We got to chatting, and I figured he might as well wait here for me to finish," Mary added before setting down her floral shears and frowning at Kaylee. "Why do you look as if you've seen a ghost?"

Kaylee hesitated, not sure if she was overreacting to the menacing call. She bided her time, setting her tote on a side counter and reading over the order sheet before glancing back at Mary.

Mary raised an eyebrow. "I can tell you're upset about something. Spill it, missy."

Kaylee smiled, her friend's intuition warming some of the icy feeling she'd had since the caller had disconnected. Her gaze flitted between the sheriff and Mary. "You're right. On my way here, I got a call from an unknown number that spooked me."

The sheriff put his hands on his utility belt. "Do you want to file a report?"

Kaylee shook her head. "I don't have any real information. The number was restricted, and the person didn't threaten me. She just tried to scare me, I think."

"What did she say?" Eddie asked.

"She said she saw what I did," Kaylee recalled. "And she

told me not to mess things up, though I'm not really sure what that meant."

The bell on the shop's front door chimed. "I'll get that while you two talk," Mary offered. "Then I'll come back and finish Susan's bouquet." She hurried out of the room with Bear on her heels.

Eddie focused his attention entirely on Kaylee. "What is it that you did?"

Kaylee grimaced as the reality of what she'd been planning to do—and the fact that she now had to explain it to the island sheriff—sunk in. "I took a glass from Madrona Grove to test its contents for snakeroot."

"Why?" Eddie asked, and Kaylee knew that the single word could have any number of meanings. If she had to guess, it was probably genuine curiosity mixed with a significant amount of rebuke.

"I've spent a fair amount of time filming over there, and I'm . . . suspicious of some of the people involved in the show."

"That makes two of us," Eddie muttered. "What does this glass have to do with your suspicions?"

"Vanessa Vanguard clearly doesn't like the producer, Sawyer, but she's still been making him all these juice drinks. Yesterday and today, I noticed him looking rather ill. It turns out that he's diabetic, but I just wanted to be sure Vanessa wasn't poisoning him." She shook her head. "It sounds silly to say it out loud."

"If you suspected this, why didn't you tell me? You could have asked for one of my deputies to collect it." The sheriff sighed. "As it is, this evidence was obtained illegally, so I wouldn't be able to use it in court."

"It's not technically evidence," Kaylee said. "But if I do find black snakeroot in it, it would give you a lead to start investigating Vanessa."

Sheriff Maddox ran a hand through his hair. "Vanessa Vanguard, huh? Do you really believe she killed Forester? That she's been slipping poison into the producer's juice?"

Kaylee slumped against the worktable. "No I don't. I think, deep down, I wanted to test the juice to make sure she's innocent, not to pin anything on her."

"I agree that she's probably not to blame here," Eddie said. "Mrs. Vanguard may have not appreciated Gabe Forester's behavior on set, but it was a drop in the bucket compared to the other grievances my team dug up on him. He'd upset more than a few people, to say the least. He most recently accepted a new role in a television series on one of the big networks. This season of *Restaurant Restarts* was going to be his last. Without Gabe Forester, the show would be dead."

"But it's continuing to film now," Kaylee argued. "It can't be that dead."

The sheriff shrugged. "My gut tells me money is the motive. People have money invested in the show, and they won't see a return on it if the host leaves and ratings fall. They'll lose sponsors."

Mary reappeared at the door to the workroom. "Knock, knock," she said aloud. "Can I come in?"

"Of course." Kaylee glanced at the half-finished bouquet on the worktable. "I'm sure Susan would prefer a finished arrangement. I'm sorry. I should have been working on it while you were in the other room."

Mary waved her guilt away. "I'd much prefer that you and Eddie talked out whatever was making you feel unsafe."

"Besides, half of a Mary Bishop creation is better than anything whole I'd get over in Eastsound," Eddie said as the front door bell jingled the arrival of another customer.

"My turn," Kaylee told Mary. "See you later, Sheriff." She headed for the sales floor, as confused as ever. One customer turned into dozens, however, and she didn't have another moment to think about the case until after closing time.

Mary had gone to the farm to do some prep work for the wedding decorations, so the shop was quiet while Kaylee swept the floor with Bear watching her lazily from a nearby cushion. As she moved the broom, she thought about the sheriff's theory that the motive behind Gabe's murder was money. Did Eddie have a suspect in mind? An investor or sponsor, perhaps? Maybe an executive at the network had recruited someone in the crew to plant the snakeroot bulb on his drink. Murder was often a crime of passion, but it would have taken some planning to track down a poisonous plant like death camas.

The rarity of the murder weapon still struck Kaylee as odd. *There are a million ways to kill somebody. Why use something so obscure?* It hit her as she swept dirt into her dustpan. The rarity was the whole point—because it pointed straight to Georgine Snowbird.

Shaking her head, Kaylee dumped the dust into the garbage, then decided that if her tired brain was going to continue unraveling the mystery, she'd need something to perk her up. A visit with Jessica and something chocolate would certainly do the trick.

With a promise to be back soon, she left Bear at The Flower Patch and walked next door to Death by Chocolate. The café's door opened just as she reached it, and a stocky man with strawlike hair stepped out.

"Hello, Jocko," she said, not eager to see the young reporter but too polite to ignore him.

"Hey, Kaylee." He hiked the strap of his laptop bag higher on his shoulder.

She was about to edge past him to enter the bakery when she thought of something that made her wonder. "Can I ask you something?"

He shrugged. "Sure."

"Why haven't you been sniffing around Madrona Grove for dirt on Gabe Forester's death?"

With a sly grin, Jocko leaned closer and said quietly, "Why waste time with that? The guy in charge over there offered me an even better story about somebody else if I'd leave them alone to 'mourn their loss in peace.'" He put air quotes around the last bit. "I won't give any details, but the lead he gave me is juicy. Let's just say your favorite network morning show host isn't as squeaky-clean as she acts."

Kaylee frowned. Had Sawyer fed Jocko alternative gossip to keep him from unveiling their on-set trickery? "Be careful, Jocko. I believe we've talked about how people's lives can be ruined by the words you write."

He gave her a winning grin, then waved and ambled away.

Shaking her head at the reporter's misplaced ambitions, she entered Death by Chocolate. The café's signature smell, rich and sweet, soothed her instantly when she walked in and scanned the room for Jessica. Instead, she saw Jessica's helper, Gretchen Cooper, at the cash register.

Kaylee smiled as she approached the counter. "Hi, Gretchen. Is Jess here?"

"She's in the back molding more chocolate flowers for that wedding cake," Gretchen replied. "She said not to disturb her for any reason, but I bet she'd make an exception for you."

Kaylee dismissed the idea with a head shake, remembering with a start that the Petal Pushers had canceled their usual Tuesday meeting that week because of the prep Jessica and Mary had to do for the wedding. "No, I don't want to interrupt a genius at work. I'll catch up with her later."

Although disappointed she wouldn't be able to talk through the latest in the investigation with her friend, Kaylee felt better after she'd ordered an éclair, a slice of decadent dark chocolate tart, and a handful of truffles to go—planning to text Reese to see if he wanted to share it that evening, of course. He'd been so busy at the farm, she didn't have much hope that he could make time to see her, but it was worth a shot.

She sent him a text with one hand as she walked back to The Flower Patch, a bag full of treats in her other hand. Hearing Bear barking for her, she said, "I'm coming, buddy!" Then she dropped her phone into her purse and retrieved her keys. As she slipped the key into the door, she realized that she hadn't locked up earlier. Chiding herself, she pulled the key out and stepped inside, only to find herself face-to-face with a very unexpected visitor.

"Nino!" Kaylee exclaimed, thinking she was growing tired of surprises. She quickly recovered her senses and shushed Bear, who had run over to bark at her. "I'm sorry, but we're closed."

"I'm not here for flowers," he said.

Uneasy, Kaylee remained near the door with Bear at her feet. "Well you don't have your camera, so I assume it's not a professional call. If it didn't happen on film, it didn't happen—right?" Her anxious joke fell flat.

"Right." He leveled a serious gaze on her. "Sawyer sent me to talk to you."

"Why would he send you? Message delivery doesn't seem like the kind of job a cameraman would normally do."

"Let's just say I do a lot of things for Sawyer. Our crew is like family. We take care of each other."

"So what did he ask you to tell me?" Even though she didn't want to assume the worst, Kaylee still felt a jolt of concern that Sawyer's message wasn't something she wanted to hear. "To stay away from his precious set?" Her eyes narrowed as she recalled the odd phone call she'd received earlier. "To make sure I don't mess things up?"

Nino didn't react to her comment. "Actually, to apologize on his behalf. He wasn't feeling well, and he realizes he lashed out harshly at you because of his illness. He wants you to know you're welcome back on set whenever you want."

"Why, so he can bombard me with questions about my boyfriend's past again or set me up to discover another deadly plant hidden in the garden?" Kaylee released a frustrated breath. "I doubt he was going into diabetic shock when he planted that death camas for me to find."

Nino shrugged. "Sawyer has a knack for squeezing excitement out of the most mundane situations."

"It's easy to do when you're the source of the excitement in the first place." Kaylee sighed. "I'm tired of the games, the fake drama. Why can't you guys just record life as it happens?"

"Because real life is boring," Nino said. "Drama and excitement draw viewers, and viewers draw sponsors."

"But aren't you worried about the morality of it all? These underhanded tricks, they're going to catch up with you."

"Maybe, maybe not." Nino sniffed. "You know, there's something I caught on camera today that wasn't faked. It was a forensic botanist sneaking off set with a dirty juice glass and a poisonous plant."

"Why do you think that's noteworthy?" Kaylee asked, trying to sound more confident than she felt.

"You're looking for something."

Kaylee held Nino's gaze, not sure how much to share with him—or how much he already knew. With a sigh, she realized that whatever she told him was sure to become fuel for the fire they were stoking over on the *Restaurant Restarts* set. "I'm trying to disprove a theory, not prove one."

"If you won't tell me what you're trying to find out, I may have to create an answer for the camera."

Kaylee frowned. "What do you mean?"

"The viewer could think all kinds of things when they see you taking the glass away from a clearly ill man." Nino shifted on his feet. "That you're getting rid of evidence, perhaps."

Kaylee lifted her chin. "You guys keep trying to threaten me. It won't work."

Nino laughed. "I'm not threatening you. I'm just telling you I have a job to do, and I plan to do it."

"Keeping up the show's facade, you mean?"

He shrugged. "I call it giving the viewers what they want, even if they don't know they want it."

"But it's lying."

"It's playing pretend. That's why it's called magic. People go to see a magic show knowing full well the magician is playing tricks on them. But they still go, and they still ask 'What if?' What if it's real? What if this time it really did happen? It's our job to entertain them, to hold their interest."

"I'm not sure how entertained they'd feel if they knew you were lying to them."

Nino shrugged, then edged past Kaylee to the door. "Is it still a lie if everybody believes it?"

The door closed with a soft click behind Nino, and Kaylee rushed to lock it. With a shaky breath, she leaned against the door. She felt surrounded by lies, unable to pick out a single kernel of truth from anybody over at the farm.

No, that wasn't quite right. There was one undeniable truth: Gabe Forester really was dead, and somebody had murdered him.

14

A yip from Bear broke through Kaylee's reverie, and she made a conscious effort to shake off the uneasy feeling that Nino's visit had given her. She took a few steps from the door into the shop, and the stairs to the second floor came into view, reminding her of what she'd locked away up there earlier in the day—the juice glass from Madrona Grove. "I just need a little bit longer, Bear," she told her dog. "Then we'll go home."

She set her dessert bag on the counter along with her purse, then ascended the stairs. Bear followed her, but when she pulled out her keys to the spare bedroom that housed her microscope, he knowingly trotted into her office to curl up on the cushion in there. She unlocked the bedroom door and entered the room, flicking on the overhead lighting and bathing her experimental greenhouse plants in more illumination than their targeted grow lights offered. She watered her plants methodically but absently, her mind on other matters entirely.

Once she'd tended her plants, she retrieved the dirty glass from the miniature refrigerator under the worktable and got to work prepping slides and other tests to determine whether or not the juice contained any trace of death camas. A short time later, she had her answer. Vanessa hadn't tried to poison Sawyer, at least not with this batch of juice.

Kaylee was both relieved and, frankly, embarrassed. The more she thought about it, the more foolish she felt for suspecting the chef of trying to harm Sawyer—or Gabe, for that matter.

But who had?

The sheriff's mention of money motivating Gabe's murder

came to mind. Someone associated with the show stood to lose a lot of money when the host moved on to another job, but was that really a good enough reason to kill him?

It is if they can make more money selling a show about a murdered host.

Kaylee grimaced at the thought. Sawyer was clearly willing to pull a lot of dirty tricks to keep *Restaurant Restarts* exciting, but would he really resort to murder? After all, he'd been scrambling to find a new path for the show after Gabe's death, and if he wanted to profit from dramatizing the murder, he would have put all his efforts into milking the crime for all it was worth. Instead, he'd tried to drum up excitement via other avenues. *Including rehashing Reese and Gabe's so-called feud.*

Not wanting to get bogged down in thoughts of Reese's romantic past, Kaylee turned off the overhead lights and left the room, locking the door behind her. "Come on, Bear," she called. "Time to go home."

Bear's claws tapped merrily on the wood floor as he came to join her on the landing, then followed her down the steps. As they reached the first floor, Kaylee heard her cell phone ringing from inside her purse, which she'd left on the counter. She rushed over and caught it just in time. "Hello?" she answered.

"Hello, dear!" Bea Lyon's voice was a welcome sound to Kaylee's ears, and she grinned instantly.

"Hi, Grandma. How are you?" Kaylee grabbed her purse, then held the phone between her ear and her shoulder to clip a leash on Bear's collar.

"I'm fine. Just missing my girl. What's new in Turtle Cove?"

"Why do I think you already know the answer to that question?" Kaylee led Bear out the back, locked and double-checked the door, then crossed the back lot to her car.

"I may have heard a few things," Bea admitted. "I do still

have a lot of friends on Orcas Island, and they've been keeping me well informed about *Restaurant Restarts* filming there. Is it true that you were out at Madrona Grove the day that poor man died?"

"Unfortunately, yes." Kaylee started the car, and the phone transferred automatically to the hands-free function. "It was a difficult day, and things have only gotten weirder."

"How so?" Bea asked.

Kaylee spent most of the drive to Wildflower Cottage recapping the activity at Madrona Grove, both leading up to and occurring after Gabe's death. She mentioned how Matt had seen the show as a saving grace when the Vanguards' nest egg ran out during renovations, and how he'd felt so compelled to make a go of the farm and restaurant because he and Vanessa were struggling to make their dream of parenthood a reality. From there, she told Bea about how nothing on set had been what she'd expected, from the fact that Gabe only dropped in briefly to film his parts to the underhanded way Sawyer was trying to drum up drama. Finally, she explained how Georgine Snowbird had been involved in the happenings at the farm, both her warning of curses and her application of dried snakeroot to Matt's bite. That led Kaylee to recount her experience finding death camas planted in the garden where she was certain it hadn't been before.

As she was wrapping up, she expressed again her disdain for Sawyer's underhanded tactics when it came to fabricating stories on set. "It's so dishonest, Grandma. It makes me wish I wasn't associated with the show."

"I can understand that, dear," Bea said. "But it sounds like, at the very root of things, you're helping a couple realize their dream. The show won't be there forever, but one can hope that the farm to table restaurant will be a big success. Everything else is just noise."

"The Vanguards aren't the only ones whose dream relies on this circus." Kaylee navigated onto her street, driving cautiously in the gathering dusk. "Another couple, Josh and Savannah, are supposed to get married there as part of the show's finale." She shook her head. "I just hope nothing else bad happens that prevents their wedding from going forward."

"If anyone can get to the bottom of things, it's you," Bea said confidently. "Keep your chin up, dear, no matter how tricky it gets. You've always been able to dig up the truth when no one else could."

"Thanks, Grandma," Kaylee murmured, her heart lifting a little.

"Now I'm afraid I have to go. I have bridge club this evening with Lucille at the Binghams' house. You should call Reese and see if he feels like coming over and making you feel protected for a while. Better yet, I think he ought to put a ring on your finger and make you feel protected all the time."

"You and Mary are just awful. Say hi to Aunt Lucille and the Binghams for me," Kaylee said, smiling at the thought of Bea and her twin sister playing cards with other friends in their retirement community.

As she pulled into the Wildflower Cottage driveway, she caught sight of something that widened her smile exponentially. Reese was sitting on her front porch steps, a pizza box from The Right Slice resting on his knees. She realized she hadn't checked her messages since texting him about dessert, and the surprise of finding him there delighted her.

"You're a sight for sore eyes," she said as she and Bear emerged from the car.

"I heard what happened at the farm earlier," Reese said, getting to his feet while Bear sprinted over to greet him. "Want to talk about it over pizza?"

"I'm all for the pizza part." Kaylee exhaled tiredly. "But can we talk about anything but the farm, just for tonight?"

"Honestly?" Reese grinned. "I thought you'd never ask."

Kaylee's break from thinking about the farm didn't last long, unfortunately. Reese forgot his wallet at Wildflower Cottage after their impromptu pizza-and-a-movie night, so she offered to save him some time by delivering it to Madrona Grove the next morning.

Though the skies were now merely a soft gray, heavy clouds had dropped buckets of rain overnight, and Bear made a point of splashing in one or two puddles on the way to Kaylee's car. Glad she had thought to bring a towel, she dried off his paws before letting him into the back seat. "I hope you can stay out of the mud at the farm," she chastised him lightly, then gave him a final pat on the head before climbing into the driver's seat.

The road to the farm was slick, and the gravel driveway leading up to the barn was riddled with ragged potholes full of murky water. The barnyard appeared to be deserted when Kaylee parked and climbed out of her SUV. But as she clipped a leash to Bear's collar, she noticed a tall, thin woman she didn't recognize near the door of the production trailer.

"Kaylee, what are you doing here?" Vanessa asked, appearing at the barn's side entrance, a door that led to the kitchen.

Kaylee glanced over and waved at the chef. "Good morning. I'm here to bring Reese his wallet."

"Husbands, I tell you." Vanessa smiled and shook her head. "They'd lose their heads if they weren't attached. Come on in. I think he's in the dining room."

Experiencing a frisson of electricity at Vanessa's accidental reference to Reese as her husband, Kaylee felt a smile tug at her lips as she turned back to pick up Bear, planning to carry him into the barn so he wouldn't pick up any mud. As she gathered him in her arms, she scanned the area. The woman she'd just seen had seemingly disappeared, and Kaylee wondered fleetingly where she'd gone. *Probably into one of the other trailers.*

The kitchen smelled wonderful, as usual, and Bear sniffed appreciatively at the warm air. Kaylee saw four dishes of food under a warming lamp and two plated salads on a counter nearby.

"It smells amazing in here," Kaylee said, her stomach rumbling despite the fact that the hour was much closer to breakfast than dinner. "Are you experimenting with new menu items?"

"We're shooting Josh and Savannah's food tasting." Vanessa pointed to the microphone she already had clipped to her apron. "We rescheduled since it was supposed to be filmed the day Matt got bitten by the snake."

"How is Matt doing, by the way?" Kaylee asked.

"Well enough to be out milking the cows at four this morning and feeding the chickens at six as usual." Vanessa chuckled. "He honestly felt silly after that whole scene in the cow pasture. I think he was just so surprised to have been bitten by a snake that he went into shock."

"That's entirely possible." Kaylee frowned, recalling how Matt had described the snake. "Did Matt remember anything else about what it looked like? He said it had stripes like a coral snake, but that seems odd. I've never seen anything bigger than a garter snake here."

Vanessa knit her brow in uncertainty for a moment, then shrugged. "Maybe somebody's pet got loose. Or maybe it's *the curse.*" She wiggled her fingers and smirked, then glanced at the wall clock. "I'd better get out to Suzy's makeup station. She's set up in the barn in case it starts raining again."

Still carrying Bear, Kaylee followed Vanessa into the dining room, where stands of lights and three cameras were set up around one of the new varnished barnwood tables that had been delivered that week. She scanned the room for a sign of Reese but didn't see him, so she trailed Vanessa to Suzy's makeshift makeup station at the front counter.

Josh stood a few feet away, tapping at his phone screen with his thumbs. Savannah was perched on a barstool, her hands resting on her lap. She wore a blue gingham dress that might have seemed like a cheesy nod to the farm atmosphere on another woman, but her beauty made it seem fitting rather than forced.

"It'll be your turn in a minute, Vanessa," Suzy said as she arranged Savannah's natural blonde curls with a comb.

"You have such gorgeous hair," Vanessa said brightly to Savannah. "I always wanted curls like that, but this mop is straight as spaghetti." She gestured to her fine, golden hair, which was gathered in a high ponytail. "How are you going to do it for the wedding?"

Savannah beamed as only a bride-to-be can. "I'm going to pull it to one side and let the curls cascade down my left shoulder. With the daisy crown from Kaylee and Mary on top, of course."

Kaylee smiled, appreciating Savannah's genuine enthusiasm. "You're going to be a beautiful bride."

"And you picked the most beautiful spot on the farm for your ceremony," Vanessa said. "That clearing in the orchard is one of my favorite places."

"Girls, I can't tell you how excited I am." Savannah balled up her fists and squealed in delight. "The arbor Reese is building is going to be amazing." She dragged out the last word, her eyes twinkling as she said it. "Mary is going to decorate it with flowers to match the ones in the barrels and the bouquets. It's just *so* perfect!"

Having visited the ceremony site with Mary during a planning session, Kaylee saw it in her mind—a glen in the woods where the sunbeams would filter through the trees to act as a spotlight on the bride as she walked down the aisle toward her groom. When Kaylee pictured the happy couple, however, it wasn't a bubbly blonde approaching her bespectacled beau—it was Kaylee herself, dressed in a simple lace gown and holding a bouquet of lavender, gliding confidently toward Reese, who gazed adoringly at her from the altar. A smile tugged at her lips as she let herself bask in the daydream for a moment longer, then she shook her head to clear it and resettled her attention on reality.

"How's your stress level?" Kaylee asked Savannah. "You seem very calm, but I know sometimes there's no helping the wedding jitters."

"Well, I'm certainly not nervous about marrying Josh," Savannah answered. "I admit that I'm a little worried about the ceremony site being finished on time, but Sawyer keeps assuring me everything is on schedule." She shrugged. "I guess I just have to trust him."

"Okay, you're set, Savannah. Next victim." Suzy barked a laugh, then beckoned for Vanessa to exchange spots with Savannah on the stool. Her eyebrows shot above her black glasses' frames as she examined the chef's face. "Did you get a facial? Your skin looks awesome."

Vanessa shrugged. "I've been standing over steaming pots all week." She laughed. "Maybe if the restaurant goes belly-up I can turn the kitchen into a spa."

Kaylee's heart twisted a little at the chef's words. The joke belied what must be a very serious fear of failure. This was all new to Vanessa—the farm, the restaurant, the TV show—and she must be near a breaking point after all she and Matt had been through recently.

"Penny for your thoughts?" Reese appeared at her side and nudged her with his shoulder. The woodsy smell of his aftershave wafted to Kaylee's nose, and she felt herself instinctively relax.

"I was wondering where you were," she said.

Reese nodded toward the wall separating them from the working area of the barn. "Just talking baseball with Matt."

"You're lucky another Dodgers fan moved to the island." Kaylee opened her tote and retrieved his wallet. "Before I forget, I believe this belongs to you."

"You're a lifesaver." Reese pulled her into a side hug and kissed her cheek. "Do you want to see the view from the second floor? We got the railing in yesterday."

Kaylee's face lit up. "I'd love to. Lead the way."

Reese took her hand and guided her past the cameras and lights to the reclaimed-wood staircase that went up to the former hayloft. As they started up the steps, he snapped his fingers. "Hang on a sec. Let me go turn the lights on up there."

Taking the stairs two at a time, Reese neared the top quickly. But as his foot reached the top step, it slipped out from under him and he released a surprised yelp.

And then he was falling straight toward Kaylee.

15

Kaylee inhaled sharply, accidentally squeezing Bear in her fright. He squirmed and jumped out of her arms, then they both raced up the steps to where Reese had landed halfway down the staircase.

"Reese, are you okay?" She saw that his face was screwed up in pain. "What hurts?"

"My pride," he said through clenched teeth as he flipped over to sit on the step. He rubbed his lower leg through his jeans. "And I think I'm going to have a massive bruise on my shin."

"What happened? Did you miss a step?"

Reese shook his head. "I slipped in some water up on the landing."

"Why was it wet? Did they just mop the floor?" Kaylee glanced up the staircase and saw a few drops of water drip from the ceiling onto the second-floor landing.

Reese tilted his head back to gaze at the roof. "It looks like the roof is leaking, but I don't know why. It's a brand-new roof, and I finished that section myself."

Suddenly, Sawyer was at the bottom of the staircase. "Don't move. You could have other injuries. Somebody call an ambulance!"

"I don't need an ambulance," Reese said. "It's just my leg. I whacked it on the step when I fell." He winced as he tried to stand, so he sat back down. Bear nudged Reese's hand with his black nose, and soon Reese was rubbing the dog's head.

I guess there are worse ways to distract someone from their pain. Kaylee knelt by Reese's other side and placed a hand gently on his shoulder. "Maybe we should call the paramedics."

"I've been telling you all that this place is cursed!" Georgine stepped forward from the shadows, joining the crowd of bystanders who had gathered at the bottom of the stairs. Kaylee was surprised to see the woman on the farm again.

"What are you doing here?" Sawyer barked at her. "Haven't you done enough?"

"I came to see how Matt is faring after suffering that snakebite the other day." Georgine's tone was even, but her eyes were narrowed into slits. "I have lived on Orcas Island all my life, and I have spent most of it in nature. But I have never seen anything resembling the snake he described. Does that seem strange to you, Mr. Hawkins?"

"I'm sure you'll tell me it's just your spirits causing trouble, trying to get everyone off their land." Sawyer sneered. "The only curse on this land is you."

"No, Sawyer, it's you." Reese climbed to his feet and started limping down the steps. Kaylee grasped his elbow and tried to support him as best she could.

The producer whirled around. "Excuse me?"

"You know what I'm talking about." Reese's voice was strong, though he was favoring his bruised leg. "That's a brand-new roof. Why would it all of a sudden spring a leak a few days before the wedding?"

"It was windy last night," Sawyer said smoothly. "Maybe it ripped off a few shingles."

"And what about when the electricity in the kitchen shorted out last week? Did the wind do that too?" Reese huffed in frustration. "I'm not blind, Sawyer. I know you're sabotaging this renovation so you can capture your precious drama on camera."

"Let's not go throwing around accusations." Sawyer's gaze flicked toward the cameras set up nearby. Quite predictably, Nino was behind the closest one, focusing the lens on the showdown between producer and carpenter. "Maybe this place really is cursed."

"You're the curse," Reese repeated.

"Are you embarrassed that you tripped on your own two feet?" Sawyer taunted.

Kaylee felt Reese stiffen beside her, and she squeezed his elbow to express her support.

"I'm sorry, but I can't let you continue to put me or my crew—or anyone else around here—at risk with your games. I quit." Reese started for the exit, but it was slow going with his bum leg.

"What?" Savannah shrieked, her face stricken. "You can't quit! You'll ruin my wedding!" She burst into tears and raked her hands through her hair, mussing the careful style that Suzy had just created. Josh pulled her into his arms and rubbed her back.

Reese glanced toward the couple and appeared about to say something, but he remained silent and continued toward the patio door. Kaylee backtracked a few steps to collect Bear. She stooped to grasp his leash, then hurried to catch up to Reese, but she had to stop in her tracks to make way for Suzy as the makeup artist stormed across the dining room toward the bride.

"Savannah, calm down," Suzy commanded. "You're messing up your makeup and getting it all over Josh's shirt."

"I don't care." Savannah raised her face from Josh's chest, revealing a mess of runny mascara and smeared lipstick. "This wedding is a disaster, and all you can think about is my makeup?"

Suzy shook her head in anger. "I'll never be able to fix those puffy eyes. You people expect too many miracles." She stomped away, mumbling aloud in a mimicking voice, "Suzy, make me look younger. Suzy, make me look prettier. Suzy make me look sick. Suzy, make me look . . ." Her voice trailed off as she burst through the restaurant's front door.

Vanessa, who had been hovering near the makeup station, stepped forward and grasped Kaylee's elbow. "Is Reese okay?"

"That depends on your definition." Kaylee had never seen Reese this worked up, and she could tell that any stress relief he'd felt during their date the previous evening had completely vanished. "I'll go check on him."

Figuring correctly that Reese had returned to the working area of the barn, Kaylee found him sitting on a bench near the milking stalls, which were currently empty. Although the floor was swept clean, barnyard odors certainly remained, and Bear sniffed at the wooden stanchions, probably wondering where their bovine occupants had gone.

Kaylee slumped down next to Reese on the bench, a sudden wave of relief hitting her. "I'm so glad you weren't hurt worse. You could have—"

Reese put his arm around her. "I'm fine. Don't think too hard about it."

"How can I not?" Kaylee shivered despite the warm spring morning. Bear came and sat beside her feet, resting his body against her. "This place is dangerous. Gabe is dead, Matt got bit by a snake, and you could have broken your neck falling down those stairs. I don't blame you for quitting."

Reese sighed heavily. "I don't *want* to quit. I feel like everyone is counting on me: Vanessa and Matt, Josh and Savannah. The only person I don't care about pleasing is the man in charge, and he's the one who's causing all the trouble."

"I wouldn't be so sure," came an unfamiliar voice from the barn entrance.

Kaylee squinted toward the door, but the bright light outside obscured the person's identity. "What do you mean?" she asked.

The unknown newcomer stepped closer, and Kaylee recognized the woman she had seen outside the production trailer earlier. Instead of answering Kaylee's question, she held up a bundle in her hands. "I brought you an ice pack from the kitchen."

"Thanks," Reese said hesitantly, accepting the ice pack she offered. "I'm Reese, and this is Kaylee."

The thin brunette smiled wanly. "Where are my manners? I'm Deborah Newton."

"Are you a crew member?" Kaylee asked. "I don't remember seeing you around before."

"No, I'm just a lookie-loo from Steely Bay," Deborah said. "I've been hearing about all the excitement here, and I thought I'd stop by and check it out for myself. Even though I went to college in L.A., I've never been on a television set before. Certainly not one where someone was murdered."

"It's supposed to be a farm," Reese said grumpily, causing Kaylee to wonder if he was in more pain than he was letting on.

Kaylee raised her eyebrows at Deborah. "It sounds like you don't think the producer is to blame for all the bad things happening here. How would you know?"

Deborah chewed on her lower lips for an indecisive moment. "I'd bet that Georgine Snowbird is to blame, personally," she said finally.

"So you believe in the curse?" Kaylee asked.

Deborah laughed, a brittle sound that echoed against the wooden barn walls. "Not at all, although it sure does make for an interesting story. But Georgine is fiercely protective of the land of her people. She'll do anything to make sure the past is preserved. And I mean anything."

"You can't possibly think Georgine murdered Gabe Forester to convince everyone that this land is cursed." Kaylee shook her head at how absurd it sounded when she said it out loud. "Georgine is a healer by trade. Why would she put people at risk with these stunts?"

Deborah merely shrugged noncommittally and backed toward the door. "I only know what I've heard. And if you think the stuff she's pulled so far is bad, you have no idea what that woman is capable of." A moment later, she stepped through the door and was lost in the glare of sunlight outside.

"Thanks for the pep talk, lady," Reese muttered as he continued to hold the ice pack to his shin.

"Want me to take you home?" Kaylee offered.

He inhaled and exhaled deeply, then shook his head. "I need to apologize to Savannah. She shouldn't pay the price for me being unable to control my temper."

"I think she was most concerned about the arbor you're building not being finished in time for the wedding."

Reese visibly brightened. "It's almost done. I can finish it and the last few barrels for Mary's water arrangements by Saturday without a problem."

"What about the rest of the project?" Kaylee asked. "What else is left?"

"Aside from fixing the roof—again? Not much, actually." Reese rolled his eyes. "Just repainting the barn yellow for Sawyer."

"I think it's perfect the way it is, and I bet the Vanguards think so too." Kaylee kissed his cheek. "So, you got to tell Sawyer off and you still pretty much finished the job. I'd say that's a win."

"You sure know how to make a guy feel better." Reese beamed, then the smile turned slightly bashful. "Would you mind doing me a favor, though?"

"Sure. What is it?"

"Will you go see if Savannah and Josh are willing to come out here and talk to me? I'd rather not limp back into the barn and have my apology caught on film."

"Of course." Kaylee stood up and held out Bear's leash.

"Can you watch Bear? I don't want the tension in there to make him uncomfortable."

"It's the least I can do." Reese picked Bear up off the ground and set him on the bench. The dog gazed lovingly at Reese, his tongue lolling out as he panted blithely. "I'm always up for some quality time with my favorite pooch."

Kaylee walked around the side of the barn to the patio door. Josh and Savannah were huddled together at one of the tables. Feeling a rush of sympathy for the couple, Kaylee dug a packet of tissues out of her tote and went over to hand them to Savannah.

"I'm so sorry about everything," Kaylee said. "And so is Reese. I was just talking to him near the milking stalls, and he has good news for you."

Savannah sniffed. "He does?" She pulled a tissue from the pack and blew her nose. "I could use some good news right now."

"That's for sure." Josh nodded toward the dining room. "The cops just showed up."

"What?" Kaylee peered through the glass door. Nick was talking in a cluster with the Vanguards, Sawyer, and Georgine while Garth and Nino milled around near the cameras. With a quick goodbye to the couple, she hastened into the building.

"Well somebody called to report that Ms. Snowbird is trespassing," Nick was saying. "And I'd like to know who it was."

"It wasn't me," Matt said. "Georgine hasn't done anything wrong as far as I'm concerned. She's our neighbor, and she's welcome here anytime."

"Hasn't done anything wrong?" Sawyer yelped. "What about trying to poison you after you were bit by a snake? She's hardly an innocent."

"She was trying to help him," Vanessa argued. "If there's anyone I'd report as trespassing on my land, Sawyer, it's you."

Sawyer scoffed. "That woman and her so-called *curse* is behind everything going wrong here. I'd put money on it."

"There is nothing 'so-called' about the curse on this land," Georgine said. "The only thing that will erase a curse is a blessing, but I have seen very little in the past weeks to indicate that is possible."

"What about the wedding?" Matt asked. "Doesn't that count as a blessing?"

Georgine shook her head, her expression remaining grave. "No. A blessing cannot be planned."

"What a kook." Sawyer sneered. "I regret the day I ever invited you to take part in the show."

"So are you the one who called, Mr. Hawkins?" Nick asked. "You sound like you have it in for Ms. Snowbird."

"It wasn't me," Sawyer answered. He glowered at Georgine, who responded with a steely glare of her own. "But I wish it was."

Garth stepped forward and cleared his throat. "Deputy? I have something to show you that you might find pertinent."

Everyone's gaze went to the show's director, who shifted uneasily and exchanged glances with Nino, who remained otherwise passive.

"It's Garth Sloan, right?" Nick asked, placing his hands on his hips. "What is it you want me to see?"

"I suppose I should have showed it to you when I first saw it, but . . ." Garth hesitated, then gestured to the computer monitor set up behind the cameras. "I think it's better if you just take a look."

"What are you doing, Garth?" Sawyer growled.

Without answering, Garth led Nick to the computer, and Kaylee and the Vanguards joined them while Georgine remained rooted in the same spot. Garth bent over the computer and, with a few clicks of the mouse button, brought up an application that populated the screen with more than a dozen small boxes, each with a different view of the farm taken from an odd angle.

"You have hidden cameras set up," Kaylee said, stunned. She hadn't thought she could still be surprised by anything on this set. With a quick scan of the ceiling, she spotted at least two cameras screwed into the beams.

Garth shrugged. "We don't want to miss anything."

"I don't suppose any of your hidden cameras captured someone garnishing Gabe Forester's drink with a poisonous plant bulb, did they?" Nick asked wryly.

"No," Garth said, "but they did capture this." He clicked on a box showing what appeared to be the rear exterior of the barn. He rewound the footage until the lighting dimmed and the camera switched into a night mode, which gave the film a spooky cast. When the time stamp read just after midnight, a figure in a striped garment came into view, their face obscured by a hat. Garth continued reversing the footage until the figure disappeared again, then he hit play.

"That's out back," Vanessa said, pointing beyond the staircase that led to the former hayloft.

Kaylee felt ice seeping into her veins as she watched the mystery person carry a ladder to the side of the building, set it up, and ascend the rungs. A short while later, the figure reappeared climbing down the ladder, a crowbar tucked into their belt.

"Whoever that was, they climbed up to the roof over the second-story dining room," Vanessa said. "That's where Reese slipped in the water this morning. This guy must have ripped up the shingles with that crowbar."

"That's not a guy," Matt said, pointing to the screen, where the person had grabbed the ladder and turned to leave.

Kaylee gasped. Matt was right. The person's hair was braided, and her striped coat had an eagle emblem on the back.

Every face snapped toward Georgine, who stood still and straight a few yards away.

"Can you explain this to me, Ms. Snowbird?" Nick called.

Georgine's gaze flicked toward the monitor. "No. I cannot explain it."

"There's more," Garth said, a hint of eagerness in his voice. He brought up footage from another camera, this one showing the garden. He reversed a few days to more night-vision footage, and hit play.

Kaylee's stomach dropped as she watched the same woman walk into the frame, hover over a small patch of dirt for a few moments, then move out of view. "That's where I found the snakeroot plant," Kaylee said, her heart in her throat. But something was off about the image—she just couldn't put her finger on what.

"I have another one that shows her messing around with the wiring in the kitchen," Garth said, though he was quickly drowned out by Sawyer.

"It's that Snowbird woman," Sawyer declared, his expression smug and his voice triumphant. "Deputy, you must arrest her. She has clearly been trespassing and causing criminal mischief."

"That could be me for all you know," Kaylee said. "I have long, dark hair too." Nick shot her a look that indicated she probably shouldn't offer herself up as a potential suspect, and she resisted the urge to stick her tongue out at him.

"But do you own that ugly coat?" Sawyer sneered. "I heard her tell you it used to be her mother's."

"Is that true, Ms. Snowbird?" Nick took a few steps toward Georgine. "Is your coat an heirloom, or is there more than one?"

Georgine breathed in deeply, then exhaled. "I don't believe I want to answer that here in front of these people."

Kaylee saw Nick wince before he said, "Then I'm afraid we'll have to continue this conversation in an interrogation room at the sheriff's station."

16

Feeling unmoored by the events at the farm, Kaylee drove to Turtle Cove in a cloud of gloom while Bear sat with his paws at the window, occasionally barking at seagulls as they dipped and dove over the sound. During a pause at a stop sign, Kaylee glanced at her carefree little dog and couldn't help but crack a smile. *At least one of us is unaffected by all the drama.*

Kaylee's spirits lifted further as she stepped into The Flower Patch's workroom and caught Mary humming and swaying to the oldies radio station as she tucked *Bellis perennis* and *Delphinium elatum* into mason jars tied with twine. Kaylee smiled at the pretty contrast of shapes and colors between the round white daisies and the spikes of blue delphinium and thought they'd be the perfect centerpieces for the dinner tables at Josh and Savannah's reception. Assuming Reese's optimism wasn't misplaced, the young couple would still have the wedding of their dreams at Madrona Grove, complete with Mary's gorgeous floral designs.

Mary stopped dancing when Bear trotted over to her and turned hopeful eyes on her. "Good morning, handsome," she cooed, rubbing his silky head. She shifted her gaze to Kaylee. "You look like you could use some coffee."

Kaylee released a mirthless laugh. "I certainly could. I'll get you one too, then I've got a lot to tell you."

Thirty minutes later, two dozen completed centerpieces filled the table and Kaylee had caught Mary up on the strange events that morning at the farm between sips of coffee.

"So, did Nick actually arrest Georgine, or did he just take

her down to the station for questioning?" Mary asked. "There's a big difference."

"He didn't handcuff her or anything," Kaylee said. "She went willingly, even though Vanessa and Matt were arguing that they didn't want to press charges against her for trespassing."

"And you're sure it was her on the video?"

"Whoever was in the video was wearing Georgine's coat, and it's a family heirloom."

"I don't know Georgine well, but what I do know of her doesn't make me think she'd ever be caught sneaking around private property playing pranks in the middle of the night." Mary shook her head. "Something doesn't add up, but I can't figure out what it is."

"Join the club." Kaylee sighed, then checked the clock and saw it was time to open the shop for customers. Whether the math added up or not, she'd have to wait until later to work on the equation.

Cold sweat beaded on Kaylee's forehead as she stumbled through the grove of Pacific madrones, squinting into the dark shadows and tripping on roots and stones jutting up from the rocky ground. The lower-hanging branches of the Arbutus menziesii *reached toward her like skeletal arms, and the trees' waxy green leaves clustered so tightly in the overhead canopy that not a speck of moonlight filtered into the woods.*

She wandered for what felt like an eternity, fearful that she was getting farther from her destination rather than closer to it—but where was she supposed to be going? Finally, a pinprick of light appeared far ahead, and she clumsily traversed the uneven forest floor in pursuit of whatever lay ahead. The spot of light grew larger and larger until she reached a clearing with a bonfire built in the center.

As Kaylee stepped into the glen, she noticed that each tree encircling the fire had the face of someone from Madrona Grove carved into its trunk. She approached the closest one, which was a depiction of Matt Vanguard wearing a surprised expression. The next tree was carved with Vanessa's likeness, though instead of surprise, her face showed distrust. Kaylee continued making her way around the circle, examining each face: a stoic Georgine, a smug Sawyer, a smirking Nino, a scowling Suzy, an irritated Garth with a bushy beard made of bark.

At first, Kaylee didn't recognize the woman depicted on the final tree. The eyes were closed, and tangles of carved hair obscured part of the face. Kaylee edged closer. As she neared the tree, she tripped over a root, and her gaze shot to the ground while she got her bearings. When she refocused on the tree, the carved woman's eyes were open, and her identity was unmistakable: Deborah Newton, the stranger from Steely Bay . . .

Kaylee awoke with a start. The dim light of dawn was just peeking around her bedroom curtains. Although Kaylee's eyes were open, Deborah's visage remained like a ghost clouding her vision. Who was she, really? Plenty of islanders had filtered in and out of the farm since shooting had begun, hoping to see how television shows were filmed, to be part of the magic. But Deborah's presence at Madrona Grove the previous day had seemed different somehow, and Kaylee was nearly certain she hadn't just been a "lookie-loo from Steely Bay," as the woman had described herself.

Feeling trapped by the tangle of sheets around her legs, Kaylee extracted herself from her bed, careful not to disturb Bear, who lay snoring softly near the pillows. She padded into the kitchen and started the coffee maker, all the while wondering about Deborah's connection to the farm.

Her thoughts were interrupted by her phone chirping an alert. While the coffee dripped into the carafe, she unhooked the device from its charger and smiled when the screen showed a text message from Reese. *Plan to finish arbor and barrels by this afternoon. Free for dinner? I can bring takeout to The Flower Patch if you and Mary will be working on wedding flowers.*

Kaylee had a better idea, and she hurriedly typed out a response. *Mary and I can't do much more with wedding flowers until tomorrow. How do you feel about a dinner date in Steely Bay?*

A few moments later, the phone chimed again with Reese's answer. *Is it a dinner date or are we investigating?*

You know me too well, Kaylee wrote back. *It's a little of both. Is that okay?*

Wouldn't miss it, Reese told her. *I'll pick you up after closing.*

With a smile, Kaylee poured herself a cup of coffee and watched the sky turning pink through the kitchen window, wondering just how she'd gotten lucky enough to find a guy like Reese.

"Ready to tell me why we're driving all the way to Steely Bay?" Reese asked as he drove past a sign signaling a turnoff to Moran State Park. He and Kaylee were a little more than halfway across the island, and they'd finished catching each other up on their respective days.

"I know, it's about as far from Madrona Grove as we can get," Kaylee said, absently petting Bear's head as he snuggled in her lap. "Not exactly the obvious place to follow clues about Gabe's death."

"I'm sure you've got a good reason."

Kaylee nodded. "Remember that woman at the farm yesterday, Deborah Newton? I don't think she was just there to watch the show being filmed. Something about her strikes me as suspicious, so I thought we could try to learn more about her."

"You didn't find anything about her on the Internet?"

"I didn't have a chance to check," Kaylee admitted. "Mary and I were busy all day completing shop orders for the weekend so we can focus on the wedding. I didn't even make it up to my office."

"Want to try now?" Reese slowed his truck and turned east toward Steely Bay on a forested two-lane road. "Maybe you can learn something that will tell us where to start our search."

"Good idea." Kaylee pulled her phone out of her purse, trying not to disrupt Bear in the process. When she woke up the screen, she groaned. "No service out here."

"I suppose it adds to the adventure," Reese said, grinning. After she put her phone away, he reached over and held her hand. "I'm glad we get to spend the evening together, no matter what we're doing."

"Same here. Aside from our impromptu date the other night, I feel like we've barely spent any time together lately—even though we've spent a lot of time in the same place."

Reese turned serious. "I originally agreed to the job at the farm because Matt hired me. There wasn't this crazy time crunch that the TV show put on things. And then Sawyer came in and took over, and all of a sudden everything had to be done in days, not weeks or months. Add to that all the drama he's been stirring up, and . . ." He sighed. "I'm sorry, Kaylee. I never imagined it would come between us. I promise I'll make it up to you."

Kaylee squeezed his hand. "There's no need to apologize. It hasn't come between us. I just miss you. But you're more than welcome to make it up to me if you think it's necessary."

"I will." Reese paused, then opened his mouth to speak again, but Bear interrupted him with a bark at another dog being walked along the sidewalk. Instead of continuing his thought, Reese simply said, "We're here."

They'd reached Steely Bay, a quaint, seaside town with cobblestone lanes leading to a small inlet of water sharing the village's name. Cute cafés and boutiques mingled with small real estate, dentist, and insurance offices, and all the businesses featured similar clapboard siding and well-maintained signage. Street-side parking spaces were surprisingly plentiful on this warm spring evening, and Reese soon found an open spot big enough to accommodate the pickup.

Kaylee leashed Bear, then climbed out of the truck. As she set him down on the sidewalk, she noticed that sea glass and shells had been embedded in the concrete, adding another dash of seaside charm to the little town.

"I'm surprised there aren't more people out and about," Reese said when he joined Kaylee on the otherwise empty sidewalk.

"It is a weeknight," Kaylee reasoned, then frowned. "I hope I can find somebody to ask about Deborah."

"Do you really think she's involved in Gabe's death?" Reese asked while they strolled down the street.

Kaylee shrugged. "I won't know until I talk to her."

Just ahead, the door of a jewelry shop called The Treasure Chest opened and a woman emerged, then locked the door behind her and dropped her keys into her large purse.

"Excuse me," Kaylee said as she approached her. "May I ask if you know someone here in Steely Bay?"

"Sure." The middle-aged woman pushed her red hair out of her eyes and gave a friendly smile, though the end-of-day sunbeams backlighting Kaylee and Reese caused her to squint slightly. "Who are you looking for?"

"Deborah Newton. She's tall and thin and has dark hair." Before Kaylee could finish her description, the woman's smile straightened into a tight line.

"Sorry, I can't help you after all." The redhead pivoted on her heel and strode to a sedan parked at the curb. She got in and sped away, leaving Kaylee somewhat dazed by the abrupt change in demeanor.

Kaylee watched the car disappear around the next corner. *Did that mean she didn't know Deborah—or didn't want to help me?*

"Let's keep walking," Reese suggested. "This town isn't any bigger than Turtle Cove. We're bound to find someone who knows Deborah."

"I hope so."

Stopping and starting occasionally so that Bear could sniff a lamppost or a flower planter, they moved on until they came to a café called Caught Bread Handed. Photos of their menu offerings hung in the window. Each one was named after a famous criminal, such as a sub sandwich called Bologna and Clyde and a salami-stuffed Al Calzone.

"How about this for dinner?" Reese asked. "We can take it to go and sit in that park at the end of the street that overlooks the bay. I see some picnic tables."

"That sounds perfect," Kaylee said as the sea breeze tousled her hair and the sunlight warmed her skin.

"You can stay out here with Bear, and I'll run in," Reese suggested. "What would you like?"

Kaylee scrutinized the menu, chuckling to herself at the names. "I'll have the Lucky Lettuciano salad, I think."

"A fine choice," Reese said. "It's the Sleep with the Fishes sandwich with Dillinger sauce for me. I'll be back in a few."

While Reese went into the restaurant, Kaylee stayed on the sidewalk, letting Bear lead her wherever his nose guided him.

A few doors down, two women stepped out of a tea shop named Just a Teas. The ladies, one blonde and one brunette, chatted and laughed as they walked toward Kaylee. When they neared her, they greeted her warmly.

"Hello," the blonde said, then she spotted Bear. "What a cute dog. May I pet him?"

"He'd be disappointed if you didn't," Kaylee answered. While the blonde woman petted Bear, Kaylee asked, "Do either of you happen to know Deborah Newton, by any chance?"

The dark-haired woman suddenly looked as if she'd eaten a slice of lemon. "Fortunately, I do not."

The blonde woman gave Bear a final pet, then stood up. "I've definitely heard of her, but I don't actually know her, thank goodness."

"Any idea how I can find her?" Kaylee managed to ask through her confusion over their strange reactions.

"Maybe check the town records," the blonde said. "Sorry, we can't help you."

As the women hurried down the street, their earlier laughing turned into conspiratorial whispering, and Kaylee grew even more puzzled.

The front door of Caught Bread Handed opened, and Reese stepped out with a large paper sack. "Ready?" he asked.

Kaylee furrowed her brow. "I suppose."

"What's the matter?"

"I asked two more people about Deborah Newton, and they practically ran away from me."

Reese gave a wry laugh. "The guy at the counter almost didn't serve me when I asked if he knew her. I wonder what she did."

"No kidding." Kaylee sighed, then reached her hand out to Reese and flashed a smile. "I guess if nobody wants to talk to us, we'll just make this a plain old date night."

"Works for me." He took her hand and they followed the street to where it dead-ended at a seaside park.

A few other people were in the park, walking their dogs, jogging, or riding along the network of paths on their bicycles. A cluster of empty picnic tables were set up around a tile-bottomed fountain. Reese and Kaylee quickly chose a spot with a nice view of the bay beyond.

Reese opened the bag to serve the food. "Sorry, Bear. I don't have anything for you."

"Don't feel too bad. I fed him at the shop before you picked us up." Kaylee opened her purse and pulled out a dog biscuit. "But I'll give him a little treat so he won't feel left out."

She made Bear do a couple of easy tricks, then handed over the cookie, which he crunched happily while Reese and Kaylee ate their dinner. Aside from an occasional comment about how good the food tasted, they ate in companionable silence.

When they had finished eating, Reese took their trash down the path to a receptacle. While he was gone, an elderly man with a cane ambled up to Kaylee.

"Cute dog," he said. "A dachshund, right?"

Kaylee smiled. "Yes, his name is Bear."

"Oh, a big name for such a little guy. He must have a big heart." The old man's eyes twinkled in delight.

"The biggest. He has lots of love to go around."

"May I sit down and pet him? I don't have a dog any longer. And at 93, I'm too old to take in another one."

"Of course." Kaylee waved for him to take a place on the bench beside Bear.

"Haven't seen you around before," the man said as he rubbed Bear behind the ears.

"My name is Kaylee. My boyfriend and I are just here from Turtle Cove on sort of a whim."

"What kind of whim brings you all the way over to this side of the island?"

Kaylee bit her lower lip, not wanting to elicit the same reaction in this kind man as she had in the other women she'd asked about Deborah. But she didn't want to be dishonest either, so she finally said, "We came to find a resident of Steely Bay. Deborah Newton."

Kaylee studied the man's face for a reaction. He grew quiet but gave an affirmative nod.

"Do you know her?" Kaylee asked.

He nodded again. "Oh yes."

"Did something happen that has made her whole town dislike her?"

Reese returned as Kaylee was finishing her question. He greeted the man and introduced himself.

"I'm Hal Boulder." Hal shook Reese's hand. "Welcome to Steely Bay. Although I wish you had come for different reasons. I'm guessing you didn't receive the warmest of welcomes from anyone you mentioned Deborah Newton to."

"We didn't know what to expect coming here, but we certainly didn't want to offend anyone," Kaylee said. "I hope we didn't."

Hal waved a hand. "They'll get over it."

"Can you tell us what happened?" Kaylee asked. "If it's not too upsetting, of course."

"At my age, nothing fazes me." Hal pointed toward the regal bluff towering out over the bay. "You see that bluff?"

"It's beautiful," Kaylee said, marveling at the natural splendor.

Hal nodded. "It is. It's also an old Native American burial ground. And will remain untouched forever, much to Deborah Newton's disdain."

"She doesn't want that land protected?" Kaylee frowned. "I'd think preserving it would be a good thing."

"It would, unless you owned the land and it was taken from you." At a nudge from Bear, Hal went back to petting him. "And you had planned to build timeshare units on it."

Kaylee returned her gaze to the top of the cliff. "They were going to build up there?"

"It's a perfect spot, don't you think?" Hal asked. "Would have brought a lot of tourists to our little town."

"What happened?" Reese asked, sitting across from Hal.

Hal shrugged. "They started digging and quickly found the first of the human bones there. It became quite the sensation—even national news crews came to the island. Through it all, Deborah was very vocal about what she said was her right to continue developing the land. It made a lot of people mad, and lots of different groups got involved. Finally, the government came in and shut the operation down and protected the land. Deborah sued, but even with funding from a silent partner, she ran out of money to fight it eventually. She was left broke, with unusable land." Hal paused, then said, "Let's just say she treated people pretty poorly after that. She's made herself a thorn in everyone's side."

"Why do you think that is?" Kaylee asked.

"She felt no one stuck up for her," Hal replied. "They left her to fight alone. Especially with that Native American woman persuading everyone to protect the land. She was relentless in her picketing and hollering about curses."

"Curses?" Reese repeated and caught Kaylee's gaze.

Kaylee straightened up, an uneasy feeling settling in. "This woman . . . her name wouldn't happen to have been Georgine Snowbird, would it?"

"That sounds familiar." Hal tilted his head. "Why? You know her?"

Kaylee did her best to keep a neutral face. "I met her on the *Restaurant Restarts* set."

"What's *Restaurant Restarts*?" Hal asked.

"A television show that's filming at Madrona Grove over on our side of the island, near where Georgine lives," Kaylee explained. "You haven't heard of it?"

"Can't say that I have," Hal said.

"I'm surprised," Reese said. "The host died during filming. I'd expect that news would have made its way over here."

Nodding in agreement, Kaylee added, "Deborah knew. She's been over to watch the filming. Georgine has spent a lot of time at the farm too."

Hal scoffed. "I hope not at the same time. Deborah hates that woman. I couldn't imagine the two of them being within a ten-mile radius of each other without one of them ending up dead."

Kaylee winced at Hal's words, then found herself wondering if he was unintentionally on to something.

Had the feud between the two women somehow resulted in Gabe's untimely death?

17

After a little more small talk, Hal bid Kaylee and Reese good night and left their picnic table. Kaylee watched the man walk away, thankful he'd taken the time to tell them about Deborah Newton's history in Steely Bay and fretful about what her past meant for the present trouble at Madrona Grove.

"You look like you could use a stroll to clear your head," Reese said, rising from his seat and holding out his hand. "Come on, it's nearly sunset."

Kaylee smiled and took his hand, then tugged gently on Bear's leash. Not needing much prompting, the little dog hopped off the bench and led them down a path that meandered toward the shoreline.

After a few minutes, Kaylee felt much more relaxed, and she could sense the same in Reese. "You seem a lot calmer now," she said. "I guess it was good to get off our side of the island after all."

Reese nodded, his gaze focused on the splashes of pink and orange beginning to appear in the clouds. "I honestly hadn't realized how stressed I was working on the renovation at the farm until I stopped."

"But you did an amazing job," Kaylee said. "Your workmanship was incredible. I knew you were talented, but I didn't realize just how much. I'm honestly a little surprised you don't take on more big jobs."

"Big jobs mean big pressure." Reese inhaled deeply, then released the breath. "It's hard to explain, but I'd rather unclog Lydia Mack's sink or rewire Bina Hall's light switch or clean out Walter Spiece's gutters any day. Making my client's lives easier, fixing their problems, helping them get on with their day—that's what I find rewarding."

"I hadn't thought about it that way before, but it makes perfect sense. Feeling useful would certainly be more rewarding than repainting a barn yellow on Sawyer's whim." Kaylee nudged Reese with her shoulder. "I can tell he rubbed you the wrong way from the get-go. I'm not surprised you got fed up with being part of the show."

Reese paused as if gathering his thoughts before replying. "What annoyed me the most was how he kept trying to dredge up Gabe's and my so-called feud. It was ancient history—or at least I thought it was. Having Sawyer regularly reminding me of Nicole got me thinking about her more than I have in years."

"Oh?" Kaylee stiffened, worried that she wouldn't want to hear whatever else Reese had to say.

"And all that thinking? It helped me truly realize just how lucky I am that she broke off our engagement when she did." Reese sighed. "Nicole was always more ambitious than me, not to mention a very competitive person. At first, I thought it was a great quality, that we balanced each other out. But nothing was ever good enough for her—including me, I guess. She wanted me to become this big-time contractor building luxury homes, but all I ever really wanted to do was help people. When she finally came to grips with the fact that I was content being an 'ordinary guy,' she dumped me."

They had paused at the water's edge to watch some gulls swoop and dive for their supper. The sky was aglow with fiery splashes of pink, red, orange, and purple, a rainbow celebration of another day's ending.

Kaylee turned her face up to meet Reese's gaze. "You're not ordinary, Reese. You've helped more people as a handyman on Orcas Island than you ever would have building overpriced homes for rich people in California. I'm sorry that Nicole couldn't see the greatness of that."

"I'm not sorry." Reese brushed a strand of hair away from Kaylee's forehead. "If I'd married her, I never would have moved here. I never would have met you. And I'd never have known what it felt like for someone to appreciate me for who I really am, not who that someone thinks I should be." He paused with his hand on her cheek, and the skin warmed under his touch. "I love you, Kaylee Bleu."

Tears prickled Kaylee's eyes, and she blinked them away as she beamed back at him. "I love you too, Reese."

With nothing more needing to be said, he kissed her.

"Thank goodness there's going to be a wedding today," Mary said Saturday morning as she and Kaylee carried cartons of fresh flowers from the shop's delivery van toward the glen at Madrona Grove. As promised, Reese had completed the arch and delivered it to the picturesque site where Josh and Savannah's ceremony would take place. "I wasn't always sure it was going to happen with all that's been going on around the farm."

"Everything has been on track since the other day," Kaylee said. "No more evidence of a curse since Nick took Georgine away."

"I'm still not convinced that she was the one behind all the pranks. Or Gabe's murder, for that matter."

"Me neither." Kaylee frowned. "I asked Nick about Georgine, and he told me that the Vanguards won't press charges and Sawyer won't give them access to the footage, so they had to release her. He wouldn't tell me whether or not he thinks she's guilty though."

Kaylee had caught Mary up on what she and Reese had learned about Deborah Newton in Steely Bay, but with all the wedding preparations, Kaylee hadn't had much chance to put more thought into the matter. After working late into Friday evening with Mary, she'd barely had enough energy to feed and walk Bear before she'd dropped into a dreamless sleep.

Bear, of course, didn't share Kaylee's level of exhaustion, and he'd turned sad puppy-dog eyes on her that morning when she'd left him behind to drive to the farm to prepare for the wedding. Reese had gallantly offered to mind The Flower Patch all day since he was done at the farm, and part of his offer included picking Bear up later and bringing him along to the shop. The thought of her two favorite guys spending all day together in one of her favorite places brought a smile to Kaylee's lips.

"Still smiling about Reese's big confession?" Mary teased as she set her cartons of daisies beside the arch and opened the top one. "It's a long time coming, if you ask me."

Kaylee blushed, but her smile widened. "We haven't even been dating that long. And I was smiling about Bear, if you must know."

"Mm-hmm," Mary hummed knowingly, then stood back and assessed the arch. "I think we should start in the middle and work our way down both sides." She grimaced. "We forgot the stepladder at the shop."

"I'll go grab a ladder from the barn," Kaylee offered. "There's one near the milking pens."

"Thanks, Kaylee." Mary pulled some floral shears out of the canvas tool belt she wore. "I'll start trimming daisies while you're gone."

Kaylee trotted out of the orchard and past the cow pasture to the barn. As she walked along the side of the building, she stumbled and just barely caught herself against the wall before she tumbled to the ground. Embarrassed, she glanced around and was grateful to see that all the crew members in the vicinity had been too busy with their own tasks to notice her. Realizing her shoelace had come undone, she bent down to tie it. As she did, she heard Garth talking to someone nearby.

"You've done more than enough," the director was saying, his voice gruff. "You need to get out of here before anybody sees you."

Who is he talking to? Kaylee jumped to her feet and rounded the corner. By the time she cleared the building, Garth had vanished . . . and Georgine was hurrying into the woods that led toward her property.

"Georgine!" Kaylee called, starting to jog after the woman.

A sudden hand on her arm stopped her.

"Kaylee, thank goodness," Suzy said, her voice sounding desperate. "Savannah needs her daisy crown for pictures, like, five minutes ago."

"Just give me a . . ." Kaylee's words trailed off as she watched Georgine's eagle coat disappear into the woods. She'd never catch up to her now. Why had Georgine been here? What business did she have with Garth that he didn't want anybody to know about? With a sigh, Kaylee faced Suzy. "The crowns and bouquets are in my van, out near the glen. Let me take a ladder to Mary, then I'll be right back with the bridal flowers."

"Thanks, doll." Suzy winked. "Meet us in the makeup trailer."

After a quick stop to grab the stepladder from the milking stalls and a hurried explanation to Mary about her next errand, Kaylee drove the delivery van across the farm to the row of trailers set up behind the barn. She parked, grabbed the boxes of daisy crowns, and headed for the makeup trailer. Balancing the boxes between her arm and her knee, she knocked on the door. Suzy appeared a moment later and let her in.

"Oh Savannah, you're gorgeous," Kaylee gushed when she saw the young bride standing at Suzy's station, the bright lights on the mirror illuminating her glowing face. Her ethereal gown featured a lace-trimmed bodice, delicate cap sleeves, and several layers of tulle cascading from a satin belt around her waist.

Savannah beamed. "I can't believe it's finally my wedding day," she squealed. "Is that my daisy crown?"

Kaylee nodded, handing the boxes to Suzy. "One for you, and one for the flower girl. Is she here?"

"Not yet," Savannah answered. "Everybody else is getting ready at my parents' house in Eastsound. They'll be here closer to the ceremony, but Sawyer and Garth said they needed me early to film some extra footage."

With an uneasy feeling, Kaylee hoped that the extra footage they were shooting wouldn't be in pursuit of any more ratings-driven drama. *Poor Savannah has been through enough this week.*

Fortunately, any concerns Kaylee might have had about the wedding encountering bumps in the road, planned or otherwise, were for naught. The next few hours sped by as if the day was a movie on fast-forward.

Once Mary and Kaylee finished setting up the flowers at the ceremony site, they moved on to decorating the restaurant's dining room, where the reception would be held. When they were done, the room radiated sophisticated country charm. Even a frazzled Vanessa took a break from cooking to peek in from the kitchen and express her delight before returning to preparing a high-end dinner for more than a hundred guests.

Each of the custom-built tables featured a blue-and-white checked runner that showed off the rustic finish of the barnwood tabletop—thankfully Sawyer had never mentioned painting them yellow again. Votives in jam jars flanked Mary's pretty daisy-and-delphinium arrangements, and each place was set with the fun juxtaposition of fine china and a mason jar water glass. Instead of favors, the couple had left a calligraphed note at each place saying that they'd donated money in their guests' honor to the Orcas Island Historic Preservation Council, which Kaylee thought was a lovely idea.

Kaylee and Mary were just putting the finishing touches on the water-barrel gardens set up near the front door when Jessica burst in. Her normally sleek hair was disheveled, and a splotch of frosting on her cheek matched several on her work apron.

"Jess? What's wrong?" Kaylee asked as she and Mary hurried to their friend's side.

"It's a disaster," Jessica groaned. "I was driving the bakery van over and went around a curve, and there was a turtle crossing the road right around the bend. I had to slam on my brakes to avoid hitting him."

Mary grimaced. "Yikes."

Kaylee peered into Jessica's face. "Are you okay?"

"I'm fine, and the turtle is fine—but half of the cake boxes landed on the floor." Jessica's face took on a pained expression. "I'm afraid to check them."

Mary grabbed Jessica's hand and patted it reassuringly. "Kaylee and I will come with you. Strength in numbers."

As it turned out, Jessica didn't have as much to worry about as she'd feared. The second tier, featuring peanut-butter chocolate-chip cake, was slightly dented, but with some "frosting spackle," as Jessica called it, the tier would be fine and should still support the vanilla top section. The other tiers were mostly unharmed, though a few of the molded-chocolate daisies had been pushed into the buttercream.

Mary and Kaylee helped Jessica carry the cake boxes and other supplies she needed to the tablecloth-covered dessert station set up against a side wall. As they entered the dining room for the last time, Jessica commented on the remarkable transformation.

"I'm seriously impressed at how fast they renovated the barn," Jessica said admiringly. "And they must have finished just in time. I can still smell the floor varnish."

Mary and Kaylee exchanged glances. "It was touch-and-go for a while," Mary said, clearly holding back a smirk.

"And these barrels—wow!" Jessica gushed. "I know you described them to me, but to see them in real life is a whole other thing. I'm absolutely amazed."

"They were all Mary's idea." Kaylee studied the array of candles and daisies floating around a centerpiece of ethereal water wisteria and spiky blue pickerelweed, but found nothing to tweak.

"This whole place is going to look magnificent tonight," Jessica said with a smile. "If I know you two, the ceremony site looks just as fabulous."

18

The ceremony site certainly did look gorgeous, Kaylee was proud to say. Freshly showered thanks to the Vanguards letting them use their farmhouse's bathroom, Kaylee, Mary, and Jessica had donned cocktail dresses and joined DeeDee at the glen to watch Josh and Savannah exchange vows. A burlap runner edged in ribbon was laid between rows of white folding chairs, and a mason-jar flower arrangement matching those in the reception hall hung on a shepherd's hook at the end of each row.

It was a joyful ceremony, with more than a few tears shed as the young couple pledged their lives to each other, and everything went off without a hitch. Soon, all the guests would be making their way across the barnyard to the barn to continue the celebration, so Kaylee and Mary hurried ahead of the crowd to light the candles in the barrel gardens.

"Hand over your phones, please," a bored-sounding Suzy instructed as they approached the restaurant's front door. She held a black plastic bin about the size of a bushel basket.

"You're taking our phones?" Mary asked skeptically.

Suzy shrugged. "Garth and Sawyer's orders. They don't want any visuals leaking before the show is broadcast."

Kaylee and Mary exchanged glances, then complied and went into the barn. Any misgivings they had were soon forgotten as guests began filtering in. They stayed near the front door and had the pleasure of hearing everyone's charmed reaction as they entered the newly renovated dining room.

"Can you believe the difference?" one man asked his wife.

"I remember when they sold pumpkins out of this barn," another guest said with a laugh.

"I can't wait to see this place on *Restaurant Restarts* when it airs," a young woman told her date.

At that comment, Kaylee realized that she had gotten so used to being around the show's cameras that she hadn't even noticed Nino and his crew filming that day. Thinking back, she knew they had been present for the wedding preparations and ceremony—even now, there were still cameras set up to capture every angle of the reception, not to mention the hidden cameras everywhere—but they'd had the grace to remain unobtrusive during Josh and Savannah's special day. *I can see how those reality TV stars get used to this lifestyle . . . but it doesn't mean I could.*

An older gentleman in a gray suit matching the groom's walked up to Kaylee. "Excuse me, miss," he said. "Could you please help me find my table? They wouldn't let me wear my glasses for the photos, and I'm afraid I've misplaced them."

"Of course," Kaylee agreed, then led the man to a small table holding place cards lined up in neat rows. "What's your name?"

"Preston Rutherford." He chuckled. "I'd like to think they haven't stuck me at the back."

"You must be Josh's father." Kaylee scanned the cards and found his amid several others bearing the same surname.

"Proudly so, yes," he answered. "That boy is what they call a good egg."

"I agree." Just then, several details clicked into place in Kaylee's mind. "Mr. Rutherford, you're on the Orcas Island Historic Preservation Council, right?"

"The president, actually, until they kick me out." The man's jovial demeanor took on a slightly more somber cast as he nodded. "Why do you ask? I hope it doesn't have anything to do with those silly rumors about a curse on this land."

"Not directly, no. Although I gather you worked with Georgine Snowbird in the past."

"This wedding has brought lots of folks from the past out of the woodwork," Preston said. "Georgine's heart is usually in the right place, but this curse she's cooked up is a bit *out there*, if you get my meaning."

Kaylee shifted a few inches to let another guest get to the table. "So you don't believe that two tribes fought a battle on this land long ago?"

"It's not that I don't believe it happened, but we have no historic evidence to prove it, and even less to prove that the farm is cursed or what have you." Preston shrugged. "When a native burial ground was uncovered in Steely Bay years ago, we fought tooth and nail to protect the sacred land. But Madrona Grove has been settled, farmed, lived on for well over a century. If there was anything to protect, it would have been found by now. Or it's been destroyed."

"I suppose I see your point," Kaylee said.

"Besides," Preston continued, his jovial mood returning, "when a Hollywood producer offers to pay for half your son's wedding, you don't turn it down. Even when the producer is a weasel like Sawyer Hawkins."

Kaylee furrowed her brow. "Did you know him before the show started filming here?"

Preston nearly choked on a laugh. "I certainly did, I'm sorry to say. Frankly, I'm surprised he ever agreed to set foot on Orcas Island again."

"Again? What brought him here the last time?"

"Why, that failed development over in Steely Bay, of course. Sawyer was the so-called silent partner, not that the man has ever been silent about anything. He lost millions on that disaster."

"Millions?" Kaylee repeated, her head suddenly spinning.

Rutherford nodded sagely. "Losing that kind of money? It can change a man . . . and not for the better, I'm afraid." He blinked a few times, then scanned his surroundings. "Now, where is my seat?"

Despite growing unease, Kaylee guided Preston to one of the tables closest to the dance floor.

A sweet-faced, silver-haired woman in a yellow silk shift dress stood up and bustled over. "There you are, honey," she said, taking his elbow. "I thought we'd lost you."

"No, dear. I misplaced my glasses and this kind young lady offered to help me find you." He gestured to Kaylee, who smiled a greeting.

Mrs. Rutherford patted her beaded handbag. "You gave them to me to hold, remember?"

"What would I do without you?" Preston kissed his wife's cheek, then followed her to their seats.

Despite the joyous bustle surrounding her, Kaylee found herself dwelling on what Josh's father had just revealed. Sawyer had been an investor in the failed development on Deborah's land, which meant he certainly knew her. Had she been visiting him here the other day before Garth had revealed the secret camera footage of Georgine sabotaging the farm?

With a start, Kaylee understood. Sawyer and Deborah had been concocting some sort of revenge scheme against Georgine in retaliation for her defeating their development project. Something had seemed odd to Kaylee about the footage of "Georgine" that Garth had shown them, and now she knew what: On Georgine's real coat, the one that had belonged to her mother, the eagle faced her right shoulder. On the coat in the video, however, the eagle's beak pointed left. It was a fake.

Deborah must have pulled her hair into a braid, put on the counterfeit coat, and made sure she was caught on camera planting the snakeroot and ripping up the roof. As the show's producer, Sawyer could easily have angled the cameras so that they would capture the coat but not her face—all to frame Georgine for the sabotage. But those acts seemed oddly minor compared to Gabe's murder. Kaylee still couldn't help but wonder if his death was even related to the other peculiar events on the farm.

The sound of metal on glass tinkled through the speaker system. Josh had appeared at a microphone on the dance floor, a beaming Savannah clutching his elbow. Realizing that she was standing in the midst of the dinner tables and everyone else was now seated, Kaylee hurried to the back of the room, where Mary, DeeDee, and Jessica were sitting with some men from Reese's crew at a table reserved for islanders who had volunteered their time for the farm's renovation.

"Good evening, everyone," Josh said into the microphone. "I'd like to take a moment to give special thanks to the folks without whom this beautiful day wouldn't have happened."

"And it almost didn't!" Savannah interjected gaily, eliciting laughter from the crowd.

"Savannah and I would first like to thank *Restaurant Restarts* for honoring us with this stunning wedding. You exceeded our wildest dreams."

The crowd clapped in appreciation, but Kaylee fidgeted as she tried to decide what her next step should be. Should she try to find Sawyer and get him to confess? Should she go to Georgine's house to make sure she was all right?

"I also need to thank all the islanders who have spent weeks refinishing this farm and barn," Josh continued. "Without you and your many talents, this magical evening wouldn't have happened. So thank you, Orcas Island, especially Reese Holt, The Flower Patch's owner, Kaylee Bleu, and designer, Mary Bishop, and of course, Matt and Vanessa Vanguard, our gracious hosts tonight."

While the guests clapped, Josh smiled at Savannah, deep love plain on his face. "I got to marry my best friend today, which makes me the luckiest man in this room." The groom turned his gaze back on the crowd. "However, you're about to taste Vanessa's amazing food, and that puts you at a close second." He paused for more applause. "Thank you all for coming to share the best day of our lives."

Savannah leaned toward the microphone again. "And hopefully one of the most fun days of yours. It's time to celebrate!"

Kaylee didn't feel the least bit like celebrating. She started to reach for her phone, wanting to text Nick to ask if Georgine was in custody, but then she remembered Suzy had confiscated it along with all the others.

"Are you all right?" Mary murmured as Josh and Savannah strolled hand in hand to the cake table.

"Not exactly," Kaylee replied quietly.

A smiling Vanessa handed Josh and Savannah a cake knife, and the couple clasped their hands around the handle and cut into the bottom layer, a dark chocolate cake with vanilla buttercream frosting. They took turns feeding each other bites, gazing lovingly into each other's eyes all the while. When they had finished, they went to the dance floor for their first dance as a married couple while Vanessa slid the entire cake onto a cart and wheeled it into the kitchen to be cut for dessert.

Kaylee's eyes watched the scene, but her mind remained fixed on getting to the bottom of the Sawyer situation.

"Earth to Kaylee," Mary said, apparently not for the first time.

"Sorry." Kaylee shook her head, then scanned the room. She saw Suzy and some other crew members drinking iced tea at another table, and Garth was hovering by a camera set up near the patio door, but there was no sign of the producer. "Have you seen Sawyer anywhere?"

"Not since before the ceremony, actually." Mary furrowed her brow. "Why do you ask? I'd have thought you'd seen enough of that guy for one lifetime after the way he's acted."

"I'll be back." Kaylee got up and strode toward the door before Mary could argue. Suddenly certain that Georgine was in danger, Kaylee felt compelled to go over to the herbalist's house to check on her. *If I'm wrong, no harm done. I'm just being cautious.*

When she reached the double doors, she pushed against the door on the left, but it was locked. Frowning, she tried the door on the right, but it also wouldn't budge. That was odd. Had the showrunners locked the door to prevent late arrivals from ruining the wedding footage?

She skirted the edge of the room until she reached the patio door, but it held as firm as the others. Swallowing the panic that threatened to rise up in her, Kaylee hurried to the swinging kitchen door. Inside, Vanessa and several assistants were lined up at the center island plating dinners in a rushed but orderly fashion. Not wanting to raise alarm, Kaylee walked as calmly as she could manage to the door that led to the parking area. It too was locked tight.

Her heart pounding, Kaylee tried to reason out the meaning of the locked doors as she made her way back to the dining room. But her frantic musings were interrupted by screams and a single word that turned her blood to ice.

"Fire!"

19

Kaylee pushed through the kitchen's swinging door and immediately recoiled at the acrid smell of burning cloth. Smoke filled the air, billowing up from the side of the room where Josh and Savannah had smilingly cut into Jessica's beautiful cake only a few minutes before. Now, the white tablecloth was ablaze, and the flames were spreading—and so was the panic.

Emitting terrified screams and shouts, most of the crowd rushed toward the exits while a few brave souls like Kaylee raced toward the fire. As she moved, she saw Matt struggle against the current of frightened wedding guests to reach a spot on the wall close to the fire, where he opened a glass built-in door, then shook his head. He bolted toward another spot on an adjacent wall and experienced the same thing.

Kaylee caught his arm as he was traversing the room again. "Matt—"

"The fire extinguishers are missing." Fear hollowed out his face, and the growing flames cast haunting shadows on his features. "And the sprinkler system should have been triggered by now."

"The doors are all locked," Kaylee said close to his ear, not wanting to broadcast it and get the crowd even more terrified. "We're trapped in here."

"Help! Help!" The guests closest to the doors pounded on them and yelled, but nobody came to rescue them. One man had dragged a chair over to a window and climbed up, but it was still too high for him to reach.

"Please remain calm," a reassuring voice announced over

the loudspeaker. Kaylee flicked her eyes toward the stage and saw that Preston Rutherford had picked up the microphone. "There's no need to panic, everyone."

"Oh yes there is," Matt said to Kaylee. "We've got to call for help."

"We can't. They took our phones." Kaylee was struggling to breathe, whether due to the smoke or sheer horror, she wasn't sure.

"My barn!" Matt cried, tugging at his hair. "We're going to lose everything!"

Kaylee forced herself to remain calm despite the chaos surrounding her. "No, Matt. You won't. Reese coated everything in flame-resistant varnish." She didn't mention that said varnish would have little effect if the fire were not put out, and fast. Her gaze moved from the spreading flames to the anxious crowd. "But we can't let everyone panic. Somebody could get hurt."

"Matt! Kaylee!" Mary appeared at Kaylee's side, squinting through the smoke. "None of the doors will open and the windows are too high. We're stuck!"

"I know," Kaylee answered. Considering Mary's past profession as a police dispatcher, Kaylee was certain she could handle hearing the truth. "The fire extinguishers are all gone, and the sprinkler system isn't working. I think someone planned this."

"Who would—" Suddenly, Mary gasped, then grasped Kaylee's elbow and tugged her toward the entrance. "The barrels!"

"You're a genius," Kaylee said, hope starting to replace some of her cold terror. "Matt, come on!"

Matt took charge then, quickly pairing off any guests he could recruit to carry the barrels from the doors toward the blazing dessert table. Fueled by adrenaline, Kaylee and Mary scurried from one barrel to another, sweeping the plants and floating candles out of the water and tossing them on the floor. When they'd cleared all the barrels, they grabbed one. It was heavier than Kaylee had expected, but they hauled it back toward Matt, who was instructing everyone to line up and dump their barrels one at a time so they could target the worst of the flames.

"On three," Matt commanded two of Josh's groomsmen. "One, two, three!"

The water poured out in a torrent, extinguishing the closest flames.

"Next!" Matt called, signaling for Kaylee and Mary to dump their barrel, which further dampened the encroaching blaze.

Kaylee and Mary hurried away from the fire, soon finding DeeDee and Jessica amid the crowd of frightened onlookers. Unable to hear themselves above the din of coughing and yelling, and nearly choking on the smoky air, the women remained silent, merely clutching each other as they watched the rest of the barrels being dumped.

But then Kaylee felt a rush of cool air kiss her cheeks. Hoping it wasn't just her imagination, she craned her neck to see over the crowd. A wave of relief washed over her when she saw that the restaurant's front door was now open, and guests had begun streaming out into the yard.

Desperate for fresh air, Kaylee and her friends followed the rest of the crowd outside. Fortunately, no one panicked, and the line of people escaping the barn moved swiftly and orderly. Once on the cobblestone walkway, tears of relief cooled the sting of smoke in Kaylee's eyes as she gulped in oxygen. She stepped to the side to let the men and women behind her pass, and she found herself beside Nino, who was holding the door.

"Did you let us out?" she asked between deep breaths. "Have you called 911?"

Nino patted her shoulder. "Don't worry. Help is on the way."

"Thank you." Gratitude flooded Kaylee and she hugged the cameraman. When she pulled away, she asked, "Thank goodness you weren't inside with the rest of us. We fought the fire, but . . ." She trailed off, not wanting to think about what could have happened.

"I was in the production trailer going over some of the footage from today," Nino explained. "When I came back, the door was barricaded with a two-by-four." He frowned and pointed to a bracket screwed into the barn, then to a hunk of lumber tossed on the ground.

"I think Sawyer did it."

Nino scoffed. "Nah. Even he wouldn't do something like this for ratings."

"He didn't do it for ratings. He did it for revenge." Kaylee grasped Nino's arm. "How long has it been since you've seen him? Was he on any of the footage from earlier?"

"I saw him maybe an hour or two ago." People had stopped emerging from the barn, so Nino let the door go. "We can check the tape if you want."

After a quick glance at her friends to make sure they were together and safe, Kaylee trailed Nino around the side of the barn to the row of trailers. As she stepped into the production trailer, she heard the sound of fire engine sirens in the distance. With a wince, she realized it was probably the last thing poor Savannah wanted to hear on her wedding day.

A grid of mounted flat-screen monitors covered an entire long wall of the trailer, a larger version of the grid Kaylee had seen on the computer screen the other day. "Do you have a camera focused on the front door?" she asked Nino.

"That one." Nino pointed to monitor in the bottom corner, then stiffened and squinted at the image. "That's weird."

"What?" Kaylee peered at the screen, which showed Suzy standing beside the door with a large, black container. In an instant, she realized the problem. "This isn't a live feed."

"Nope." Nino scanned the other monitors. "None of the barn cameras are live."

Chilled by the planning that Sawyer had put into covering his tracks, Kaylee swiftly decided to continue the mission she'd begun before the fire—making sure that Georgine was all right. If Sawyer was bent on revenge, she was his next likely victim. "Nino, do you have any cameras that show the area between the back of the barn and the woods?"

"Yeah, but it's not up there." Nino sat in front of a computer monitor and clicked the mouse a few times. One of the screens flickered, and a new image appeared of the spot Kaylee had asked about.

"Can you reverse it?"

"Sure thing." Nino clicked the mouse again, and the footage rewound at double speed.

After a short time, a figure in a sport coat appeared moving backward from the woods toward the barn. When the man glanced over his shoulder, Kaylee held up a hand. "Pause it there."

Nino complied, and she scrutinized the image. It was Sawyer, and he was heading for Georgine's property.

On a hunch, Kaylee pointed to a monitor showing where the fire had started inside the barn. "Can you rewind this to this morning?"

Nino clicked the mouse a few times, scrolling back through the day's recording. Thankfully, the terrifying footage of the fire went by quickly—Kaylee wasn't sure she could watch it, even in reverse. When he reached midmorning, Nino slowed the film's rewind to double speed. Workers came and went for a while, then after a lull, a woman in a familiar striped coat appeared.

"Keep going until she enters," Kaylee said.

With a nod, Nino did as she requested, then they watched the woman walk into the dining room with a knapsack on her back. She walked to the dessert table and lifted the tablecloth, then removed her knapsack. She withdrew several wadded-up cloths from the bag, then a bottle of what Kaylee assumed was a flammable liquid—perhaps the varnish Jessica had smelled? The woman doused the fabric, quickly replaced the bottle in her knapsack, and smoothed out the tablecloth, then hurried out of the frame . . . but not before Kaylee saw that the eagle on her coat faced her left shoulder. It was Deborah.

"Thanks, Nino. I have to go."

Without another thought, Kaylee bolted from the trailer and sprinted down the dirt lane that ran behind the barn. She was vaguely aware of flashing lights dappling her surroundings, but she was too focused on her objective to pay them much mind. She had to get to Georgine before it was too late.

Although it couldn't have been more than half a mile to the herbalist's house, the trek felt slow and treacherous as Kaylee stumbled over roots and rocks in the woods. She was grateful she'd had the presence of mind to pair ballet flats with her cocktail dress. The sun was still high, so she was able to navigate fairly confidently.

Finally, she emerged into the clearing that held Georgine's simple log home. The only sound was the crash of waves beyond it and the rustle of the trees behind Kaylee. Down on the shore, a solitary boat swayed in the water, but its rocking motion was the lone movement she saw.

She knocked on the front door then tried opening it, but it was locked. Shielding her eyes with her hand, she leaned her forehead against the closest window and peered inside. No movement, not even the flicker of a curtain.

Kaylee went around the side of the house to the cellar door. Not bothering to knock, she turned the knob, and it twisted with a faint squeak in her hand. She opened the door, which creaked on its old hinges. There was a dim glow at the bottom of the rickety steps, and with a flutter of hope, Kaylee thought that maybe Georgine was just working on her herbs.

"Hello? Ms. Snowbird? Georgine?" Kaylee descended the steps, each one groaning under her weight. Halfway down, Georgine's work space came into view, and Kaylee gasped.

Georgine, Deborah, and Sawyer sat on the floor against the wall, their hands and feet bound with rope. In front of them stood a sneering Garth with a revolver in his hand, its cold steel glinting cruelly in the dim light.

He shifted slightly and aimed the gun right at Kaylee.

20

Kaylee froze, her gaze locked on the gun for a moment, then shifted to the man holding it. "Garth, what are you doing?"

"What does it look like?" he growled, then narrowed his eyes. "How did you escape from the barn?" Instead of waiting for an answer, he shook his head. "Doesn't matter. These three are the ones I really wanted. The ones who deserve my revenge."

"Revenge?" Kaylee repeated. "What have any of them done to you to deserve that?"

"What haven't they done?" Garth snarled. "They cost me my life savings, the lot of them."

Kaylee glanced at Sawyer, who appeared the most frightened of the three, and the truth clicked into place. "Did Sawyer talk you into investing in the Steely Bay development?"

Sawyer's expression shot from scared to indignant in an instant. "Talk him into it? He practically begged me to let him in on the action. Silent partners in the deal of the century thanks to our old college pal Deborah. And it was a sure thing too, until this kook got involved." He jerked his head toward Georgine, whose face, as ever, remained impassive.

"None of this was my fault," Deborah argued, her voice shrill and raspy—a match for the mystery caller earlier that week. She still wore the counterfeit striped coat. "Why are you doing this to me? I was helping you, Garth!"

"So it was you and Deborah behind all the sabotage at the farm?" Kaylee asked Garth. "Not Sawyer?"

"Sawyer?" Garth was incredulous. "Are you kidding? Sawyer couldn't focus on a boulder rolling down a mountain toward him. There's no way that flighty moron could plan something like this."

"How dare you!" Sawyer cried. "After all I've done for you."

"All you've done for me?" Garth echoed. "You've done nothing but boss me around and squash me under your shoe since we met freshman year. You took advantage of me then, and you've never stopped. All you care about is having power and lording it over everyone else. It's time you finally pay the price. And you can't buy your way out of it with your trust fund this time."

"I can't believe I ever went along with your stupid plan," Deborah groused.

"What plan?" Kaylee asked, hoping that if she kept them all talking, she'd have time to figure out a way to escape.

Apparently reveling in the chance to confess his crimes, Garth grew excited, though he kept the gun trained on Kaylee. "It all started when that sad sack Matt Vanguard applied to be on our show. At first I was angry when I saw that he was from Orcas Island, but then an idea started to form. I knew Deborah was as bent out of shape as I was, so I got in touch with her and we figured out what to do—we'd kill Sawyer and set it up so Georgine would take the fall."

Kaylee grimaced. "That's—"

"Genius?" Garth finished for her.

"Some genius," Deborah said snidely. "You're the one who gave the glass intended for Sawyer to Gabe after I put that plant bulb in it."

"Making sure you were caught on camera in a replica of Georgine's coat when you did it," Kaylee guessed.

"At least somebody here isn't a complete idiot." Deborah sneered, and Kaylee was surprised at her cavalier viciousness considering the fact that she was bound just like Sawyer and

Georgine. "This guy got spooked and erased the footage before he realized he could have used it to frame the old hag."

"I admit that things got tricky after there was nothing concrete to connect Georgine to the murder," Garth said. "And I knew we couldn't try to kill Sawyer again so soon. We'd have to bide our time. So that's when we started filming all the other stuff to peg on Georgine, knowing I'd find a chance to use it eventually." His mood turned sour again. "But it didn't work. Those rat cops didn't even arrest her."

"This seems like a lot of work to get revenge for something that happened years ago," Kaylee said, aware that she was toeing a line.

"Who cares how long ago it was?" Garth snarled. "I put everything I had into that deal. I emptied my savings, remortgaged my house, even got a loan from my parents."

"None of that is my fault," Sawyer said. "I'm not the one to blame here."

"Wrong. You're just not the *only* one to blame here. Which brings us to Josh and Savannah's big day." Garth's last two words dripped with such vitriol that Kaylee shuddered. "Hopefully the worst day of their lives."

"But you've always been so . . ." Kaylee trailed off, struggling with this alarming turn of events.

"So what? Weak? Yeah, that's me. Garth the loser. Sawyer's errand boy. That's what made it so easy to carry out my plan. The whole crew is used to me just being the messenger of his crazy ideas, his ridiculous requests." Garth barked an ugly laugh. "Suzy didn't even bat a fake eyelash when I told her to collect everybody's cell phones so they couldn't call for help while I burned that accursed barn to the ground."

"But Garth, why?" Kaylee pleaded. "The barn was full of innocent people."

"Innocent? Ha! Was high-and-mighty Preston Rutherford innocent when he helped this hoodoo lady shut down our deal? He deserved to die right alongside his whole family."

"So, what now?" Kaylee asked. "Aren't you worried that the sheriff's department is going to catch you?"

"Those ineffective morons? Not likely." Garth's eyes narrowed into slits. "But just to be safe, I guess I'd better get a move on." He used the gun to gesture for her to join the others. "Not that I need to worry. When the cops show up here, it'll look like Sawyer and Deborah finally had it out over that failed deal. Deborah actually lured him here with a handwritten note, promising they'd get their revenge on Georgine together. She even tied him up like a gift for me before I got here and did the same thing to her. Of course I'll untie them once I'm done."

"You rat!" Deborah shouted. "I can't believe I ever helped you."

"Yes, I know what that kind of betrayal feels like," Garth said to her before returning his focus to Kaylee. "I was never here, but unfortunately"—he pouted mockingly at her— "you were, and you got caught in their crossfire trying to stop it. Deborah is going to disappear without a trace . . . straight into the ocean. I'll be dumping her off on my way to Canada."

At Garth's urging, Kaylee slowly moved toward the others. Wishing she could find some way to save them all, she gazed remorsefully at the terrified, furious, and solemn faces of Sawyer, Deborah, and Georgine. She paused on the last, thinking she saw a flicker of hope in Georgine's eyes as the older woman stared past Kaylee toward the stairs.

Careful not to make any sudden movements, Kaylee shifted her gaze to the open-sided staircase. She saw the glint of a shiny black shoe on the top step—an Orcas Island Sheriff's Department-issue shoe. Help had arrived.

Garth kept the gun trained on his prisoners while he fumbled in a nylon duffel set on the floor. Feeling eyes on her, Kaylee turned back to Georgine, who subtly nodded toward the drawers of herbs just behind Kaylee. Could the herbalist possibly have something in the drawers that Kaylee could throw at Garth to distract him long enough for the deputy to make a move?

Kaylee edged her hand toward the drawers, keeping eye contact with Georgine. She pointed to one, but Georgine ever so slightly shook her head. Kaylee moved on to the next drawer, and Georgine nodded. While Garth continued to pull rope out of his duffel, Kaylee inched the drawer open and hazarded a peek. Fine, red powder filled the drawer, and Kaylee had a hunch it was *Capsicum annuum*. Chili powder could be used as a pain reliever—but that wasn't what she intended with the handful she scooped up.

"Garth," she said as she approached him with what she hoped would be a distracting question. "I'm just curious—why did you release a snake on the farm?"

He stood and glared at Sawyer. "That wasn't my idea, but it was my pet king snake, Ricky. Sawyer had one of the production assistants set him free in the pasture to scare the cows, but Ricky bit Matt instead."

"Man, that was gold!" Sawyer crowed, clearly forgetting the predicament he was in.

Garth continued to glower. "Just like faking diabetes with some makeup tricks and hiring that phony investor to offer to buy the farm, it was another one of Sawyer's hairbrained ploys to amp up the drama so he'd get his precious ratings." Garth sniffed. "And now I'll never see Ricky again. He's lost, and Sawyer doesn't even care."

"Oh grow up," Sawyer shot back. "Only creeps have pet snakes."

Garth's eyes widened in anger, and Kaylee chose that moment to fling the chili powder at his face. While he screamed in anguish, she leaped behind a stack of crates to avoid being hit by any stray bullets that might escape his gun while he flailed about.

Footsteps pounded down the stairs, and an instant later, Nick's firm voice could be heard above Garth's wails. "Garth Sloan, you're under arrest for . . . well, a lot of things, apparently."

Once Kaylee heard the click of handcuffs latching around Garth's wrists, she emerged from her hiding spot and hurried to untie Georgine. When her hands were free, the herbalist cupped Kaylee's face in her hand and quietly murmured, "Thank you."

"What about me?" Sawyer asked brusquely when Kaylee had finished removing Georgine's foot bindings.

"Don't touch him, Kaylee," Nick commanded as he stood up and pulled Garth to his feet. "You see, the 'ineffective morons' of the Orcas Island Sheriff's Department have been doing their research, and it seems that some gentlemen from the government would like to chat with Mr. Hawkins about the taxes he hasn't been paying."

"Serves you right," Deborah hissed as Sawyer spluttered.

"Speaking of comeuppance, you're under arrest too, Ms. Newton," Nick said, then lifted an eyebrow at Kaylee. "You aren't under arrest, but you are probably in big trouble with somebody outside."

Once she had assisted a stiff Georgine up the basement stairs and to an ambulance waiting out front to care for her, Kaylee saw what Nick meant. Reese's shiny black truck was parked alongside the driveway. Almost as soon as she spotted it, the driver's side door burst open and Reese emerged with Bear on a leash.

"Kaylee!" he called as he rushed toward her, Bear leading the way and barking excitedly.

An instant later, she was in Reese's arms, feeling safer than she ever had, relieved that her frightening ordeal was over. She remained wrapped in his embrace for a long time, finally breaking it only when Bear put his paws on her shins and whined.

She gathered up her little dog, then fixed grateful eyes on Reese. "Boy, am I glad to see you."

"What were you thinking, running over here like that?" Reese asked, his tone at once admonishing and admiring. He shook his head. "You saved the day—again—but I think I might have suffered a heart attack trying to get to you."

"I'm sorry," Kaylee said. "I just followed my instincts. How did you find me?"

"Nick stopped by The Flower Patch to chat while I closed up, and that's when he got the call about the fire. I was worried about you and everybody else, so I followed him out here. When I got to the barn, I couldn't find you, so I asked around. Nino told me he saw you take off running into the woods after you saw video of Sawyer heading this way, so Nick and I followed you." He grinned sheepishly. "Well, Nick followed you and I followed him, but he made me promise to stay in my truck until the all clear."

"He's a wise man."

"Too bad only one of us tends to listen to him when he tells us to stay out of danger."

"I don't listen well. No one knows that better than Nick."

Another deputy cruiser crunched down the gravel lane leading to Georgine's house, its lights flashing, but its siren silent. She glanced at the ambulance, then back toward the farm. "Can they spare this ambulance? Don't they need all hands on deck after the fire?"

"Always worrying about other people's safety when you should be worried about your own." Reese pulled her into another hug, then released her. "Everyone at Madrona Grove is fine."

"Fine?" Kaylee didn't believe it. "Savannah and Josh must be freaking out. What a terrible thing to happen at their wedding."

"Actually, they're rolling with it. The sheriff is trying to keep the details of what happened under wraps—for now, anyway—so they're taking the reception outside. Matt is hanging strands of white lights in the new cowshed, and the band is moving their equipment out there. Vanessa is serving dinner and cake out of the back door of the kitchen. Last I saw them, Josh and Savannah were dancing into the sunset."

"I'm so glad." Relief flooded Kaylee again.

Reese cupped her elbow in his hand and glanced down at her green dress before gazing lovingly into her eyes. "You know, you look really pretty for someone who's helped put out a fire and chased down a murderer and who knows what else in the last hour or so."

Kaylee clamped her lips, unwilling to ruin the moment by going into detail about what had happened in the cellar. That could wait.

"So, my love, will you be my date to the wedding of the year?" Reese asked. "It's happening right next door, after all."

Kaylee looked at him askance. "It depends on one thing. Are they still filming?"

"That's what you're worried about?" Reese laughed long and hard. When he finally recovered his senses, he put on a serious expression. "I'm afraid that's a risk we'll just have to take."

21

Less than a month later, Kaylee found that she was glad Nino and his crew had kept filming the wedding.

He'd contacted the Vanguards a few weeks after the fire, apologizing for any role he'd unwittingly had in causing trouble for them and extending a very unique olive branch. With Sawyer and Garth in prison—not to mention their host being dead—*Restaurant Restarts* was effectively canceled. The police had confiscated all the show's footage, but Nino had access to a backup copy. Out of a job, the cameraman had spent several days locked in an editing room back in Los Angeles, piecing together a documentary about Madrona Grove's transformation into a farm to table restaurant.

He had sent Matt and Vanessa a copy of the final film along with his best wishes, and the couple had decided to host a viewing party the night before the newly re-renovated restaurant officially opened. Eager to finally share their labor of love, the Vanguards had invited anyone who had been involved with the project to come and watch Nino's movie with them, then share a meal in the dining room—which Reese had restored completely, leaving no trace of the fire.

Now, full of nervous anticipation, Kaylee and Reese sat in front of a large-screen TV in Madrona Grove's second-floor dining area, and it felt as if half of Orcas Island had gathered with them. The other Petal Pushers had brought their husbands, Georgine sat with the Rutherfords in the front row, and Holly and Alan were with several other deputies and first responders who had been on the scene the day of the fire. The crowd quieted as a smiling Matt and Vanessa appeared in front of the TV screen.

"Thank you all so much for coming tonight," Matt said. "We're thrilled to finally welcome you to the new and improved Madrona Grove—which I am happy to report is minus one rogue king snake. The snake that bit me was captured and transferred to a reptile sanctuary over on the mainland last week."

"I'm sure I'm not the only one who's glad for one less thing to worry about around here," Vanessa added, earning laughter from the crowd.

"This undertaking has been a rocky road, to say the least," Matt continued, "but we couldn't be prouder of what we've accomplished here. And we couldn't possibly have done it without you. Vanessa and I came to Orcas Island for a fresh start, but we found something even more precious. We found a home here."

"At times, it seemed that our dream was turning into a nightmare, but good friends"—Vanessa beamed at Kaylee and Reese—"and good neighbors"—she flashed a smile at Georgine—"helped us make our crazy dream a reality."

The couple locked eyes for a moment, then Matt winked and nodded as though encouraging his wife to say more.

Vanessa took a deep breath, then turned an even brighter smile back on the crowd. "Madrona Grove has certainly been an adventurous labor of love, but it certainly won't be our last one." She placed a hand on her belly, and Kaylee noticed that the bottom two buttons of her white chef's coat were undone. "Another dream of ours is coming true too. Pretty soon, I'll have a little sous chef running around the kitchen with me."

"Or a junior farmhand helping me with the cows," Matt added.

The crowd burst into applause and shouts of congratulations, and Kaylee felt herself swelling with happiness for the Vanguards. They'd been through so much trying to make each other's dreams come true, and now they were finally being rewarded.

As the ovation continued, Georgine rose from her seat, her

signature somber expression suddenly changed. The Native woman, whose solemn demeanor hadn't cracked for a moment since Kaylee had met her, was smiling. Georgine looked to the ceiling as though searching for something in the rafters. Then her gaze settled back on Vanessa, and her small smile quickly widened into an utterly jubilant expression.

"The curse is broken," Georgine said, placing a gentle hand on Vanessa's cheek. "A blessing has defeated it. There is no longer a hold on this land, and it is now at peace."

Vanessa pulled Georgine into an emotional hug, then Georgine and Matt shared a similar embrace while Vanessa swiped tears from her eyes. A few moments later, Georgine returned to her seat, and Matt and Vanessa held hands as they refocused on their audience.

"Now, I think we've all waited long enough to see what Nino created," Matt said, aiming a remote at the TV. "Ready or not, I present *Rebuilding Together*."

Matt clicked a button on the remote and Vanessa dimmed the lights before taking seats among their guests. Kaylee felt a frisson of nerves as the first image—tall grass waving in a spring breeze with the Madrona Grove barn in the background—filled the screen, and Reese put his arm around her.

"They say that no man is an island," narrated a soothing voice. "And on this little island, that couldn't be more accurate. This is the story of how a community came together to make one couple's dreams a reality, no matter what obstacles got in their way."

Kaylee and Reese exchanged surprised glances in the dark, and her nervous energy shifted into delight as she watched the film unfold. Instead of the drama and deceit Sawyer had tried to hone, Nino had woven the best of what he had captured into a tapestry of community-driven kindness. Missing were any hints of sabotage or curses or murder. Replacing them were scenes of Reese joking with his crew as they varnished the barn floor, an adoring Matt complimenting Vanessa's food as he tasted her latest dish, and Kaylee and Jessica gamely helping Matt milk his cows. The footage that must have been caught by a hidden camera in the milking stalls elicited hearty chuckles from the crowd.

As scenes from Josh and Savannah's wedding played on the screen, from the guests fighting the fire to the newlyweds dancing under the stars, tears sprang to Kaylee's eyes. She heard companion sniffles coming from DeeDee, Jessica, Mary, and several others in the audience, and she knew that everyone in the room was affected by the tender moments Nino had strung together so artfully.

Surrounded by the love of her friends and neighbors—people who were as much her family as her own flesh and blood—Kaylee was certain that if there had ever been a curse on this land, there was no way it remained.

YOUR FEEDBACK MEANS A LOT TO US!

Up to this point, we've been doing all the writing. Now it's *your* turn!

Tell us what you think about this book, the characters, the bad guy, or anything else you'd like to share with us about this series. We can't wait to hear from *you*!

Log on to give us your feedback at:

https://www.surveymonkey.com/r/FlowerShopMysteries

Annie's FICTION